YANKEES ON THE DOORSTEP
The Story of Sarah Morgan

SARAH MORGAN

YANKEES
❧ ON THE ❧
DOORSTEP
The Story of
Sarah Morgan

By Debra West Smith

PELICAN PUBLISHING COMPANY
Gretna 2001

Library of Congress Cataloging-in-Publication Data

Smith, Debra, 1955-
    Yankees on the doorstep : the story of Sarah Morgan / Debra West Smith.
      p. cm.
    Summary: Sarah Morgan is a spirited twenty-year-old, loyal to the Confederacy,
when Union forces arrive in Baton Rouge, Louisiana, in 1862, forcing her and her
family on a perilous journey to New Orleans. Includes excerpts from the actual
diary on which the story is based.
    ISBN 1-56554-872-8 (pbk. : alk. paper)
    1. Dawson, Sarah Morgan, 1842-1909—Juvenile fiction. 2. Louisiana—
History—Civil War, 1861-1865—Juvenile fiction. [1. Dawson, Sarah Morgan, 1842-
1909—Juvenile fiction. 2. Louisiana—History—Civil War, 1861—1865—
Fiction. 3. United States—History—Civil War, 1861—1865—Fiction. 4. Family life—
Louisiana—Fiction. 5. Diaries—Fiction. 6. War—Fiction.] I. Title.

PZ7.S644685 Yan 2001
[Fic]—dc21

00-050187

Published by Pelican Publishing Company, Inc.
1000 Burmaster Street, Gretna, Louisiana 70053
Manufactured in Canada

Contents

❖

Introduction

New York, 1896

As the three chatted over coffee in the elegant restaurant, conversation turned to the War for Southern Independence. Though thirty years had passed, it was still a subject of debate when Northerner and Southerner came together. On this occasion the gentleman from Philadelphia was especially proud of the role the Federal navy had played. "For example," he said, "consider the brilliant victory of the ironclad *Essex*. After it defeated the Confederate *Arkansas,* it was only a matter of time until the entire Mississippi River was under our control."

The fragile, gray-haired lady from Charleston had listened politely to the man, but now her clear blue eyes blazed. "Brilliant victory? I will have you know, sir, that the *Arkansas* succumbed to engine trouble and was destroyed by her own men. Only two shots had been exchanged with the *Essex* at a great distance. The Confederate sailors then set fire and abandoned the ship. When the *Essex* came round the turn, there was nothing save a burning hulk left to 'defeat.'"

The Philadelphian gravely shook his head. "I

respect your loyalty, madam, but your information is in error. I remember the newspaper reports clearly."

"Well, sir, your newspapers were in error! *I was there.* My sister and I, along with friends, watched the from the levee."

The man sighed and the woman's son, a boy of eighteen, squirmed nervously. It was unlike his calm, dignified mother to create a scene—people at other tables were beginning to stare.

The Philadelphian looked skeptical. "I am sure that reports differed with the perspective of those writing them. It is a shame that you have no proof."

"But I wrote a description of the whole affair, just a few hours after it occurred!" the woman insisted. "Early in the war I began to keep a diary, and continued until the very end; I had to vent my feelings. I have written while resting to recover breath in the midst of a stampede; I have even written with shells bursting over the house in which I sat, ready to flee but waiting for my mother and sisters to finish their preparations."

The Philadelphian rubbed his chin. "If that record still existed, it would be invaluable. We Northerners are sincerely anxious to know what Southern women did and thought at that time, but the difficulty is to find authentic evidence."

"You may read my evidence as it was written from March 1862 until April 1865," the woman impulsively told him.

When she and her son returned to Charleston, she went immediately to her tall, cedar-lined wardrobe and drew out a linen-bound parcel. It had been carefully stitched up and on the front was scratched in ink, *"To be burned unread after my death."*

"I've seen this before, Mother," said the boy. "You wouldn't let us open it."

"I thought it a record of no interest to anyone but myself," she said, digging in a drawer for scissors. "And I lacked the courage to read it—so many joys, hopes, and griefs—but perhaps it has some value."

With trembling hands she clipped the stitches and drew out five books. Two were the proper size for diaries, while the other three looked liked old ledgers. The ink had faded to pale brown on the yellowed pages, making them difficult to read. But the boy recognized his mother's clear, firm script, for the years had not changed it. He watched her read the books in the weeks that followed, copying some pages, weeping over others. She refused to let him read them, but when he was alone at night, the smell of cedar and the memory of the books haunted him.

His mother sent excerpts of her diary to the man in Philadelphia. He returned them some time later, claiming they could not be authentic. No girl of twenty could have written with such clarity and insight, he declared.

The lady was deeply hurt. She returned the books to their linen wrapping and never looked at them again. However, the son begged her to repeal the sentence of burning. . . .

Chapter 1

❖

Fire on the River

April 26, 1862

There is no word in the English language which can express the state in which we are all now, and have been for the last three days. Day before yesterday news came early in the morning of three of the enemy's boats passing the forts, and then the excitement commenced.

"Sarah!" a voice called from downstairs. "Are you dressed? Charlie sent word for us to come to the river. They are going to burn the cotton."

Sarah paused, hating to leave her journal. It had been a week since she had written anything and so much had happened. She leaned over, scribbling faster, . . . *on hearing of the sinking of eight of our gunboats . . .*

"Sarah Ida Morgan, will you please hurry?" her older sister, Lilly, called again. "You know that husband of mine. He will burn every bale of cotton in Baton Rouge before letting the Yankees have it. And he said to come *now*."

Sarah sighed, dropped the pen, and grabbed her bonnet. She met Lilly at the front door, herding out the last of her five small children. The air hummed with excitement bordering on frenzy as the citizens of Baton Rouge hurried to the river—at least everyone who had not left to join the Confederate army. Those remaining were mostly women, children, and servants, with a smattering of men. Sarah's group joined them to walk the three blocks from her home to the riverbank.

There the broad, muddy Mississippi dwarfed the flatboat waiting at the wharf for what would be its last voyage. Like the Confederate gunboats that had been sunk defending New Orleans, this vessel had a patriotic duty to perform. It was piled with bales of cotton and pine knots soaked with whiskey. When all was ready, it was towed out to the middle of the river. Sarah and Lilly anxiously watched as her husband, Charlie, and two other men set the cotton afire and jumped into a small skiff. As they rowed back to land, the morning breeze fanned the cotton into a sheet of living flame. All along the levee people shouted.

"Why did they do that?" Lilly's children wanted to know.

"The Yankees control the river between here and the Gulf of Mexico, and will arrive any day," their mother explained. "The cotton was worth a great deal of money—nearly a hundred dollars a bale. It is a terrible waste, but if we cannot sell it, neither should they."

"A year's work," added Sarah, watching as wagons unloaded more cotton from farms all around. Up and down the levee, as far as they could see, the huge bales were rolled to the water's edge, set afire, and pushed in. Each sent up its own wreath of smoke, looking like so many little steamers puffing their way down the river.

"I guess that shows what a nation in earnest will do," Sarah observed. Though her family had been against Louisiana's seceding from the Union, they were still loyal Southerners. Now it seemed that the South was fighting for its very existence. Before Sarah's father died last year, he surprised them all by regretting that he could not fight with his three sons. Still, there was comfort in knowing that their oldest sister and her husband, a Federal officer, were far away in California. And while their half-brother, a New Orleans judge, had sided with the Union, he refused to bear arms. At least the Morgan boys wouldn't be shooting at relatives.

It appeared that the cotton would take hours to burn and Sarah longed to watch, but the children were hungry and there was packing to be done. Later, after they had been fed and settled down for naps, Lilly began to collect her jewelry. It was the only thing of value small enough to carry and was more reliable for trade than Confederate notes. Sarah reluctantly helped her sister secure their mother's jewelry, then rummaged through her own drawers.

"I do not want to run," she muttered.

"What did you say?" Lilly asked.

Sarah cleared her throat. "I said that I will not move one step, unless forced away."

Lilly shushed her. "Will gunboats firing shells be sufficient to force you? Or will you wait for the Yankees to show up on our doorstep?"

Sarah tossed a tawny strand of hair that had escaped her thick bun. "I am not afraid. Let them come and find out what an excited girl is capable of. There is a small seven shooter and carving knife which vibrate between my belt and pocket, always ready for use."

Lilly was speechless for a moment. "Sarah, really . . . you talk like the boys. You have just turned twenty and should have more sense."

"If only I could have gone with them! Better to be fighting with George and Gibbes in Virginia, or even Jimmy waiting for his boat down in New Orleans. Anything would be better than sitting here like ducks. Our brothers would say that being prepared to defend ourselves makes excellent sense."

Lilly shook her head, but her lips were drawn tight and her small hands trembled as she continued to pack. It wasn't like Lilly to be sarcastic, Sarah realized. The threat of attack had placed her under a terrible strain. With Mother and their sister Miriam in New Orleans, Lilly not only felt responsible for her brood, but for a houseful of servants and Sarah as well. Giving her sister a quick hug, Sarah silently vowed not to vent her frustrations on Lilly again.

By evening, a smoky gray blanket hovered over the city. Gone were the fresh scents of magnolia and wild honeysuckle; instead the acrid smell of burning cotton stung Sarah's finely shaped nose and made her blue eyes water. But there was no time to complain. A new dispatch from New Orleans warned that enemy gunboats would pay a visit in the morning.

Lilly prepared for instant flight. "Tiche, don't forget the baby's diapers," she called to one of the servants.

"Where are we going, Mama?" asked Dellie, her oldest.

"If the town's to be burned, we shall run to the woods," Lilly called, dashing from one room to another with armloads of clothes. "Find your extra stockings now."

Alone in her bedroom, Sarah sighed. "Well, if the house has to burn, I must make up my mind to run. *But what to take?*"

Her gaze fell upon the desk, in which were stored all the letters she had ever received. It was impossible to take the whole load— there would be no room left for clothes. After a quick shuffle, Sarah chose four letters that were especially precious and placed them in a "treasure bag" she planned to tie around her waist beneath her skirt. Unknowing eyes would think she wore a healthy bustle.

Next she added the palm-sized leather diary and prayer books her father had given to her before his death. The pistol and knife were also tucked safely away. Then she piled the remaining papers on the bed and lay a box of matches on top. If the worst happened, she was ready. "At least my letters will not afford the Yankees any amusement," she muttered with grim determination. "Now, which dress . . ."

By bedtime, Lilly was put down with a high fever as the consequence of her frenzy. Sarah finished packing and tried to sleep, knowing that whatever came could be faced better if she were rested. But her ears were too well-tuned to each sound drifting through the window. Church Street would normally have grown quiet by now, except for the chirp of crickets, the boom of a bullfrog, or the occasional horn of a boat passing on the river.

Tonight, however, the men who had burned the cotton wandered the block, watching, waiting. Their voices mingled in a rough babble that made little sense. It was only noise, offering no comfort for the anxious thoughts thumping in her head.

Morning came—but still no Yankees. Sarah didn't recall sleeping, but she must have, for pale sunlight peeked through her curtains. She lay still for a moment, just listening. The day sounded like any other. What if the alarm had been false and no gunboats were coming after all?

Sarah dressed quickly, checked on Lilly, who was still confined to bed, and found the servants busy with the children. She had just poured a cup of strong Creole coffee when a knock came from the gallery. Sarah opened the front door and froze at the sight that greeted her. The gaunt face and tattered, muddy uniform were unfamiliar, but the eyes she knew.

"Will? Will Pinkney?" she whispered.

"Good morning, Sarah."

"Will, what happened to you?" she cried.

"Met the Yankees down in New Orleans. Got some more of that coffee?"

Sarah didn't know whether to laugh or cry, hug her old friend or offer him breakfast. So she did all four. Later, when the family had fed and made a proper fuss over Will, they heard about the events that had left him in such sorry condition.

It was a sad story. Will, a lieutenant colonel in the 8th Louisiana Infantry, had led his men in holding one side of the river near New Orleans as the Yankees passed through. When ammunition ran out, they had no choice but to retreat through the swamps. Will had waded over seven miles in waist-deep water before collapsing at the swamp's edge. Two of his men had revived him, but most of the five hundred soldiers were scattered, perhaps lost or dead in the swamp. Only one hundred had managed to reach Baton Rouge.

"See these shoes?" Will pointed to the thick, clumsy boots that had seen better days. "I came out of the swamp barefooted and an old Negro gave them to me. Pulled them right off his feet. "Can you believe that?" Will shook his head.

"Anyhow, we finally found a boat and landed here last night. Now I have to find a carriage and get my wife and the little one up to Clinton. They'll be safer there at Grandpa's. Then I'll go with the men to join General Beauregard up in Corinth, Mississippi. Every man who owns a gun, and many who do not, are on the way there now."

"We will conquer yet," Sarah said, trying to sound encouraging.

Will sighed. "Things have not exactly turned out like we planned."

Listening to the pain and discouragement in his voice, Sarah thought that her heart would burst. "Oh, Will, I would rather never have seen you than find you so changed!"

A familiar smile lighted his face for an instant. "Now quit, Sarah. You're supposed to be glad to see me." Then the smile faded.

This is not the Will Pinkney I parted with, Sarah thought. *Where is hearty, laughing, mischief-loving Will? He is good-looking now, which he never was before. But how I wish I could have seen the same merry, good old face I looked goodbye at, a year ago, instead of this sad, care-worn one! I'll never see my Will Pinkney again—Will that I liked, and who liked me so much; this is his ghost, for mine is dead. . . .*

Bah! I expect a man who has narrowly escaped death, and who is now running for his life to be jolly, and look extremely happy! When he comes back, and the war is over, I will see the same old Will again—only we will not meet again, I fear!

Chapter 2

❖

Invasion

"They're here!"

The words vibrated through the lengthening shadows of late afternoon. Sarah, busy in her garden, froze with trowel in midair. There had been so many false alarms in the past two weeks. The worst had been the appearance of four Federal gunboats that steamed right by! They probably had more urgent business in Vicksburg, but the few remaining citizens of Baton Rouge almost felt insulted.

"Are you sure?" Charlie shouted to the boy running down the street.

The breathless lad paused. "Yes, sir! A gunboat just dropped anchor!"

Sarah's heart seemed to "kerplop" inside her chest. So this was it. They were actually going to land this time. Sarah's mind went blank—*what to do first?*

Lilly answered that question by bursting through the door. "Bring the children in! Sarah! Tiche! Oh, hurry! The Yankees are here!"

After depositing two of her nieces inside, Sarah considered following Charlie, who had vanished down the street. Lilly's hysterics brought that plan to a halt. Despite their preparations, the comfortable two-story house with its galleries overlooking Church Street suddenly resembled a beehive. Women, white and black, scurried about packing children and supplies.

No one really knew if it would be necessary to leave, or if the "cotton burners" would make some resistance. Without cannon or militia, Baton Rouge was virtually helpless, and the few men willing to fight would probably get shot or arrested. Sarah wondered what Charlie would do, but decided against asking Lilly. Instead she slipped outside, straining to hear any sound from the river. There was only silence.

After what seemed like days, though only a few hours, Charlie returned. He fended off their questions. "Let me sit down," he protested. "Is there any supper?"

"Supper?" Lilly was incredulous. "We have been waiting here to be blown to bits, worrying about you, and wondering what to do next—and you talk about food."

"Well, I am hungry."

Sarah tapped her foot. "Charlie, *what happened?*"

"If you all will be quiet, I will tell you," Charlie announced with a wave of his hand. "There is a Federal gunboat called the *Iroquois* sitting at anchor." He paused. "A small party came ashore led by a young officer with the Stars and Stripes draped over his shoulder. He wished to speak with someone in authority about our surrender."

"What nerve!" cried Sarah. "Not even a flag of truce?"

Charlie chuckled. "The fellow was trembling in his boots. None of the city officials would come out to meet him."

"So have we surrendered?"

He snorted. "Not if they had forty gunboats lined up in the river."

"What happened then?" asked Lilly.

"The officer finally got someone to show him the way to the mayor's office. He promised not to shell the town if we let his men alone while they come ashore to buy a few necessaries."

Sarah's eyes widened. "Yankees—coming to shop?"

Charlie grinned. "Mayor Bryan told him the air is very unhealthy for Federal soldiers at night."

Sarah laughed out loud. "I should think so."

But Lilly was not amused. "What happens tomorrow? Will we have to leave?"

Charlie let out a long sigh and patted her hand. "I don't know what will happen tomorrow, dear. I truly don't. We must be ready for anything."

———— ❖ ————

Lying awake that night Sarah wondered how long her nerves, or Lilly's, could stand being "ready for anything." It was late when she finally dozed off, only to be roused by someone shaking her arm.

"Sarah, wake up."

"Wha . . . ?" Sarah rolled over and tried to open her eyes.

"Wake up, silly. We're home."

Sarah blinked. Was she awake or dreaming? "Miriam? Is that you?"

Candlelight flickered across her sister's strong, oval-shaped face and smiling blue eyes. "Of course."

Shocked to her senses, Sarah tumbled from the bed and wrapped Miriam in a hug. "How did you get out of New Orleans? Where is Mother? How is Jimmy?"

Miriam squeezed her a long moment before answering. "Mother is downstairs, and God only knows how Jimmy is. We sailed up the river under a flag of truce. I am *so* glad to be home."

The hall clock struck one as Sarah hurried down to see her mother. The sun was well up before she had heard all the stories of New Orleans under Yankee occupation. The commander, Gen. Benjamin Butler, was better known as Beast Butler for his iron-fisted rule of the city. There was cause to be thankful, however. Their seventeen-year-old brother had been ill and was not on his ship when it was attacked and sunk in port. Now Jimmy was on a train to join the fighting elsewhere.

Despite her fears and worries, having Mother and Miriam home gave Sarah new courage. Outgoing Miriam was two years older and the closest of her three sisters. Since the death of her beloved brother Harry in a duel last year, Miriam was also her dearest friend.

As the day wore on, Sarah was pleased to hear that the sailors of the *Iroquois* had stayed on board the night before. By daylight, they had taken over the abandoned Federal garrison, where their flag was quickly raised. Later that day word came that more gunboats had been sighted.

Sarah grabbed her bonnet. She started to wake Miriam from a fitful nap, then thought better of it. Miriam and Mother had probably seen enough Yankee boats. Instead she darted out the door and into the nearly deserted street. Turning the corner, she noticed the Brunot sisters up ahead.

"Nettie, Sophie! Wait!" Sarah glanced around to make sure no one was watching, then hiked her skirt and broke into a run. A lady would never show her ankles in public, but Sarah was tired of hearing about Yankees secondhand. After the unbearable days and nights of waiting for the enemy, she wanted to *see* them.

Then, as she reached the Brunot girls, four gunboats steamed into view. Sarah forgot about her skirt. Sharply etched against the sunset, the vessels were an incredible sight. Though three blocks away, the American flags flying from every peak seemed close enough to touch. Sarah swallowed hard. "As much as I once loved that flag, I hate it now," she whispered.

"I know," said Nettie. "But what can we do?"

Sarah sighed. Then her eyes brightened. "They may remove the town's flag, but what about flying our own?"

"And have your house shelled?" Nettie looked doubtful. "Besides, our family does not have a flag."

"No, no, I mean our own personal Stars and Bars. I have enough red, white, and blue silk to make a score of Confederate flags. I will wear it and dare any man to remove it."

Nettie looked from the gunboats to Sarah. "It is the only patriotic thing to do," she declared.

Together they hurried back to the Morgan house. Though excited about the project, Sarah doubted that her mother would approve and was relieved that she was still napping. After a quiet flurry of construction, Sarah and Nettie left wearing their new banners. The gunboats had disappeared, but were sure to be docking near the State House, where the Yankees were said to be making themselves at home.

"You're a bold one, Sarah," Nettie said, looking her over again. The five-inch flag with its stem tucked into her belt looked huge pinned to Sarah's petite shoulder.

"I can barely see yours." Sarah pointed to the tiny flag peeking from the folds of Nettie's skirt. "Perhaps when we set the example, others will follow."

Near the State House more than a hundred people had gathered to watch the gunboat *Brooklyn* unload. The soldiers on board stared back. The crowd stirred as Sarah and Nettie joined it. One old fellow cried out, "My, young missus has got *her* flag a-flying anyhow!"

Sarah took a deep breath and drew up to her full five feet, four and one-half inches. She had never felt prouder.

Chapter 3

❖

The Enemy

May 11th

I—I am disgusted with myself. No unusual thing, but I am peculiarly disgusted this time. Last evening I went to Mrs. Brunot's with my flag flying again. They were going to the State House, so I went with them. To my great distress, some fifteen or twenty Federal officers were standing on the first terrace, stared at like wild beasts by the curious crowd. I had not expected to meet them and felt that I was unnecessarily attracting attention by an unlady-like display of defiance. But what was I to do? I felt humiliated, conspicuous, everything that is painful and disagreeable; but strike my colors in the face of an enemy? Never!

Nettie and Sophie had them, too, but that was no consolation for the shame I suffered. How I wished myself away, and hated myself for being there, and everyone for seeing me! I hope it will be a lesson to me always to remember a lady can gain nothing by such displays.

Miriam interrupted her. "I know you are devoted to that journal, but have you noticed that it is time for church?"

"I don't feel like going today," Sarah groaned.

Miriam touched her cheek. "You have no fever. What is wrong?"

"I told you about yesterday at the State House. I am too humiliated to face anyone."

Miriam sighed. "Sarah Morgan, make up your mind. One day you are ready to defy the whole Yankee army, and the next day you crumble because they notice!"

Sarah shook her head. "You don't understand. Those men were not the ruffians we were told to expect. They were gentlemen, as refined as anyone we know. I have never liked being the center of attention—what came over me?"

Smiling at their reflections in the dresser mirror, Miriam kissed the top of Sarah's head. "This war makes everyone act strangely. Leave it be. By tomorrow we will probably have something new to worry about. Now it's time for church."

Reluctantly Sarah tied on her bonnet and joined the family downstairs. It was a short walk past the Presbyterian church to St. James Episcopal. Church Street was well named, for the bells of the Methodist and Catholic churches could be heard a few blocks in the other direction. The sight of a neighbor's rose bed and the whiff of magnolia lifted Sarah's spirits a bit. So did the fact that she was going to worship just as she had countless Sundays before. It was a comforting thing, a normal thing. How she longed for life to be normal again, where people knew what was appropriate and didn't have to blunder about making fools of themselves.

Once inside the modest wooden building Sarah quietly slipped ahead of her family into their usual pew. Hopefully their friends would be too busy welcoming Mother and Miriam home to notice Sarah or comment on her flag display the day before.

No one said anything, however, and Sarah began to relax as she sang the first hymn. *"Jesus Christ is risen to-day, Al-le-lu-ia! Our tri-umph-ant . . ."*

Suddenly the organist faltered, then stopped altogether. Her mouth hung open as she stared toward the back of the church. People murmured as they turned to look. A wall of silence fell. There was only the thud of boots on hardwood floors as a cluster of dark blue uniforms moved down the center aisle.

For an eternal moment no one in the congregation moved, or even breathed. Then little Dellie squirmed next to Lilly and whispered loud enough for all to hear, "Yankees, Mama. The Yankees came to church!"

Shock turned to outrage as Sarah watched the soldiers. How dare they interrupt a church service! Surely the citizens of an occupied city at least had the right to worship in peace.

Then a pang of fear shot through her. Was Baton Rouge about to answer for its staring crowds, ragged boys following the soldiers, refusal to surrender, *the defiant wearing of the Confederate flag?* Would they recognize *her?*

As the questions darted through her head, Sarah's eyes followed the men as they walked stiffly down the aisle. There were a dozen, all officers. She fully expected them to line up in front and state their business, but instead they turned into the empty pews in front of her *and sat down.*

A quiet gasp rustled through the congregation. What did they want? Was this their way of keeping an eye on the people? Throats cleared as the rector stepped forward, his shoe leather creaking in the expectant silence.

Like Sarah's father, the Reverend John Gierlow had once preached peace and cooperation instead of secession. It had seemed odd coming from a former officer of the Danish military. Yet as Northern oppression grew and the war gained momentum, this fair-skinned man began to support the cause of his adopted home, the Confederacy. When the bishop ordered that prayers for "the President of the United States" be changed to "the President of the Confederate States," Gierlow had complied.

Now he stood straight and calm, looking very military. Gazing toward the officers, he nodded, then motioned the organist to continue. The soldiers joined in singing, knelt to pray, then opened the prayer books resting on the pews in front of them. Around the room, people began to breathe again. Could it be that the Yankees had simply come to worship?

Mr. Gierlow called for the Psalm of the 11th day. Sarah opened her small leather prayer book and tried to concentrate on the words as he read, *"Be merciful unto me, O God: for man would swallow me up; he fighting daily oppresseth me."*

Sarah answered with the congregation, *"Mine enemies would daily swallow me up: for they be many that fight against me, O thou most High."*

"What time I am afraid, I will trust in thee," said Mr. Gierlow.

Sarah could not help but glance at the soldiers as she murmured the words of King David's ancient plea for deliverance. The psalm was well suited to the people's mood. Surely these men knew that *they* were the enemy.

"Every day they wrest my words: all their thoughts are against me for evil," whispered Sarah.

"They gather themselves together, they hide themselves, they mark my steps, when they wait for my soul."

Sarah watched the soldiers quietly reading the scriptures and began to wonder how these men whom she had never met, obviously raised in her own religion, could be her enemies? Didn't her brother-in-law in California wear that same uniform? Did it alter his place in humanity? How must it feel to enter worship with a hostile crowd so far away from home?

"When I cry unto thee, then shall mine enemies turn back: this I know; for God is for me." Sarah could not go on. When the reading was finally

over, she lay her prayer book on the wide back of the pew in front of her. She was careful not to let it stick out over the soldier's side where it might bump him when he sat down.

Gathering her full hooped skirts, she turned to sit. There was the rustle of taffeta as her hoops caught the book and gently pushed it away. Sarah saw it sliding and grabbed, but too late! With a light thump, her prayer book slipped onto the seat beside the officer.

She gasped, mortified. What if he thought she had done it on purpose? Young women were known to do such things to get a man's attention. Worse yet, what if the people behind her suspected that? There would be no end to the gossip. At least flag-waving was patriotic—flirting was not!

Sarah sank in her pew, wishing to be some-where—anywhere—else. The sermon, which she barely heard, seemed to drag on forever. But at last, it was over. As they stood to go, the officer turned to get his hat. The book lay on top of it. Sarah waited to see no more. Instead she practi-cally shoved Miriam out of the pew. The book could stay. She would have died before asking for it. Only later did she remember that her full name was printed inside.

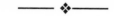

On Tuesday, the Yankees left. Every last one. The announcement came that the gunboats were to join an attack on Vicksburg. With it came threats to anyone disturbing the American flag left flying above the garrison. The town would be shelled if it met with any misfortune.

Three mornings later, Charlie came to breakfast after a quick stroll through town. His face was grim. "Well, the bait has been taken," he said. "Someone took the flag down last night and tore it to pieces."

"You were right," said Sarah. "It was a trap."

Charlie nodded. "They have been looking for an excuse to give us a lesson."

"Then nothing is safe," said Lilly. "It is just as we feared."

"What of the guerrillas that are banding together outside of town?" asked Miriam. "I hear there are nearly two thousand of them anxious for a brush with the Yankees."

"Anxious," said Charlie, "but poorly equipped. Even if they make a good show, we must leave or be caught in the crossfire."

Lilly stopped eating and bowed her head.

Sarah tried to be optimistic. "What if they are defeated at Vicksburg? I hear that Will Pinkney's regiment is up there now. Perhaps Will can sink half a dozen ships for us."

Charlie sighed. "Perhaps. But if the Yankees do return, we must assume they will make good their threat. I want all of you ready to leave for Greenwell at a moment's notice."

"Greenwell? It is such a long way, Charlie," Lilly protested. "Is that necessary?"

"You will all be safer at your mother's summer house."

"What about you?" Lilly asked.

"I will stay here and look after things."

"You mean join the guerrillas."

"I don't know yet."

Sarah joined the argument. "But there is nothing at Greenwell besides trees and springs." No place to buy food or . . ."

Charlie held up his hand for silence. "It's the best we can do now. Please be ready."

Chapter 4

❖

Attack!

May 17th

One of these days, when we are at peace, and all quietly settled in some corner of this wide world without anything particularly exciting to alarm us every few moments, and what is the Future to us now will be the Past to us then, seeing it has all come right in the end, and has been for the best, we will wonder how we could await each day and hour with such anxiety . . . and if it were really possible that half the time as we lay down to sleep, we did not know but that we might be homeless and beggars in the morning. It will look unreal then; we will say it was imagination; but it is bitterly true now.

Sarah dropped her pen and yawned. She was too sleepy to write and had been unable to sleep with Lilly's baby awake "watching the moon" all night. Sarah loved Beatrice, but her midnight squeals combined with waiting for the Yankees' return were enough to drive a sane person mad. Miriam had been wise to accept an invitation to spend the night with friends. The tension was beginning to affect the other children in the Morgan house as well. Down the hall, she heard Lilly breaking up another fight between the five- and seven-year-olds.

"They are at it early today," Sarah told the tiny yellow bird who watched her. "You know, Jimmy-boy, any woman who has brought up her children in the way they should go, and has not in the meanwhile become a shrew, or lunatic, deserves a seat in Heaven, and no questions asked!"

Jimmy chirped in agreement as Sarah pulled on the linen dress draped across the foot of her bed. She never retired now without putting out a complete set of clothes in case the alarm came at night. Ruefully, she studied the high-topped shoes, which had seen many better days. The soft English leather was worn paper thin and had begun separating from the soles. Even practical Charlie said they were not worth repairing. But with Yankee ships blockading trade, many goods were in short supply. The loose soles flapped in time with her steps going down the stairs.

"Better days are coming," she sang, trying to emulate her father. No matter what Judge Morgan's troubles may have been at his office, he left them there, always bringing home a pleasant word. No one had a right to cast gloom over the hearts of others, he used to say. Sarah knew she must try to be amiable, for everyone's sake.

"Good morning, Aunt Sarah," Dellie greeted her.

"Hello, Dellie dear. Why are you still at break-fast?"

Eight-year-old Dellie shoved the fork around her plate of grits and eggs and wrinkled her nose. "I don't like eggs. Tiche knows that and makes me eat 'em anyway."

"You be thankful to have dose eggs," said the wiry, dark-skinned woman at the stove. "Lotsa folks goin' hungry dis mornin'. Besides, dey make you grow up purty like Aunt Sarah."

Sarah patted Dellie's head sympathetically. "She makes me eat them, too, though I don't see that it has improved my looks. But I will make you a deal," said Sarah. "Clean that plate and you can go shopping with me later."

"Shoppin'?" asked Tiche. "With the Yankees keepin' our ships away, dere ain't nothin' to shop for!"

"Well, I must try, or face the possibility of running to Greenwell barefoot."

After Dellie forced down the last of her break-fast, Sarah made good on her promise. Together they sauntered down the streets, trying to pretend that Baton Rouge was not a city under sentence and this was an outing like any other. It was diffi-cult. Some stores were boarded up, their owners having already left town. Others crowded with people requesting goods in short supply— pins, cloth, tools, canned goods—anything not grown or manufactured nearby. In one store after another Sarah asked about shoes.

"Sorry, miss. We sold out of ladies' shoes weeks ago," said one proprietor.

Another just laughed at her.

"Everything we have is on the shelf," said a third.

However, Sarah was disappointed to find only one pair of ladies' slippers—both of her size number one feet would have fit into one of them. "I have always been proud of having small feet," she confided to Dellie. "I suppose pride goeth before barefootedness."

Dellie looked puzzled. "Will you really have to go barefoot, Aunt Sarah?"

"Heavens no! I was joking, Dellie. A lady *never* shows her bare foot in public. We must find something, though thanks to this war, there isn't a decent shoe in the whole city."

"Have you considered boys' shoes, miss?" the clerk asked. "We have a pair that might fit you."

Sarah groaned, then nodded. The shoes turned out to be an unbendable pair of boots a little boy might wear fishing. Though they were an inch and a half too long, she clung to them, debating. The clerk kept shuffling through boxes.

"Here! Perhaps these are small enough for your dainty feet," she announced.

Sarah studied the shoes the woman held out to her. They were cut low and made of crocodile skin with patent tips on the toes. Dubiously she slipped them on. It was a near fit."Very good," the clerk said triumphantly.

Sarah sighed and nodded. "Now I shall trudge about town in boys' shoes made of something related to a hippopotamus!"

Another tense week passed with the greatest excitement occurring in Jimmy's bird cage. Ten tiny eggs had appeared in quick succession—it seemed that "he" was in fact a "she." Since Sarah's feathered little friend had been named for her brother Jimmy, she couldn't bear to rename it. Not now, with no news of the three Morgan boys and the family expecting to hear the worst any day.

On Wednesday Charlie left before daybreak to prepare the house at Greenwell. It was seventeen miles out to the rustic cabin where the Morgans usually spent the hottest summer months. In years past Sarah had looked forward to the general confusion of packing clothes and provisions. While her brothers gathered fishing tackle and hunting equipment, she would choose books from the family library.

How different it was now. Breakfast had been dispensed with early as each family member went about her tasks. With such a large household to move, Sarah was allowed to pack only one trunk. Small piles of letters, dresses, and keepsakes lay about the bedroom as she struggled again with the decision of what to take and what to leave for the enemy. Down in the library Miriam searched for their father's important papers while Lilly went to buy supplies. Splashing was heard down the hall where Lucy bathed the baby as Sarah's mother rested.

Then, with no warning at all, Lilly burst in shouting, "Mr. Castle has killed a Federal officer on a ship, and they are going to shell!"

Her words were barely out when the boom of a cannon rattled the windows. Panic swept though the house as each reacted in her own fashion— Lilly hysterically gathering her children, Mother screaming, Miriam racing to calm her. Only Sarah stood, frozen in the moment.

"Lucy, bring the baby!" Lilly called to the maid.

"But Miss Lilly, she's all wet without a speck o' clothes."

Another cannon blast. There was screaming in the streets.

"Bring her as she is!" Lilly shrieked.

Though it was nearly impossible, Sarah tried to think clearly. There was no time to finish packing her trunk and no way to carry it if she did. Charlie had taken the carriage, which meant all would have to walk. She remembered the "running bag" she had packed weeks before and scooped her most precious keepsakes into it. Raising her long, full skirt, she secured the bag under the hoops. Then tying on a sunbonnet and grabbing Jimmy's cage, she took a final look around—Sarah Morgan was ready for anything.

Downstairs, there was bedlam. Mother was unwilling to leave, "We must save your father's papers!" she protested.

"Mother, I have already looked and can't find the important ones," Miriam explained. "We must go . . ."

"No!" Mother cried. "I will not leave my house!"

"Please be reasonable," begged Miriam. "We *must* leave and I will not go without you."

Another "Boom!" brought on more shrieking as Lilly's brood gathered at the front door.

Miriam's face grew angry and her voice desperate. "Mother, you are coming if I have to carry you!"

Watching them, Sarah felt somehow detached. She had no urge to scream, nor was she needed to take charge as Miriam and Lilly had been forced to do. Thank goodness, she had only herself to look after—and Jimmy.

She stared at the cage. How far could she carry it? The seventeen miles to Greenwell was a very long way. Anything could happen on the journey, and they could end up goodness knows where. Hunger seemed a certainty.

As if in a dream, she walked out to the back yard. The street in front was crowded with panicked women and screaming children, but Sarah hardly noticed as she sat the cage down and drew out the little bird with her hand. The tiny heart beat wildly against her palm as she gently kissed the yellow head. Taking a deep breath, she lifted both hands and tossed her friend into the sky. Jimmy gave a feeble chirp as if uncertain what to do, then flew away. Her eyes blurred with tears, Sarah leaned her head against the gatepost and cried.

Chapter 5

❖

Greenwell

The cannonading continued as all family members were accounted for and began moving down the street. They had hardly walked a square before Sarah realized that her new crocodile shoes were a poor choice for the journey. One heel was already beginning to hurt. "I must go back for another pair of shoes," she announced. "Don't wait for me. I will catch up."

"Absolutely not," declared Mother.

The others protested as well, but Sarah didn't stay to listen. "Sarah, wait!" they called. "It's too dangerous . . ."

Her sore feet limped faster. Soon she was home and digging under the bed for her worn-out hightops. Slipping her feet into them was like being hugged by an old friend. Standing in the quiet room, she paused. It was easier to think now. There were so many items lying about that she and Miriam would need. A toothbrush, comb, and of course, the powder bag—how could they stand the withering Louisiana sun without starch for their faces? But how to carry it all? Her running bag was full.

Studying her slim reflection in the mirror, Sarah frowned. Why were men's clothes made with more pockets than ladies'? They would certainly be handy today, she thought. Then her face brightened. "Yet we have something they do not," she said, quickly unfastening her blouse. With nimble fingers she untied and loosened her corset. In went the comb, toothbrushes, and powder bag. Sarah wiggled until they were comfortable. There was room for more.

Her favorite lace collar lay on the bed. She stuffed it in. The long hair tumbling over her shoulders reminded her to include a tucking comb and hair pins. "Ouch," she said, retying the corset. Glancing back in the mirror, she laughed out loud.

"Sarah!" came an breathless cry from below. It was Miriam. *What are you doing up there?*

Remembering her family, Sarah felt sheepish, but still smiled at the furious Miriam when she burst into the room. "Look at me," she said. "Do you think anyone will notice that I have put on a bit of weight?"

Miriam's face was aflame. "There are shooting at us, Sarah!"

"I was packing a few necessaries," Sarah explained, patting her ribs. "We will be glad to have them later."

"Fine," Miriam snorted, and pulled her down the stairs. Starting down the street, they discussed what the family had taken and the many things they had not. Finally Miriam stopped. "No one has an extra change of clothes. Perhaps we should get a few more."

Together they ran back a second time where Miriam threw clothes to Sarah who stuffed them in a pillowcase. It was nearly full when Mother and Tiche arrived, upset with them for taking so long.

Miriam interrupted her. "Sh-h. Listen. The cannon has stopped."

Exhausted and upset, Mother sat down. "Perhaps it is over. Perhaps we don't have to leave."

"I doubt that," said Miriam.

"Well, it gives me more time to find your father's papers," said Mother. With fresh determination, she marched into the library. Moments ticked by as she rummaged through drawers, filling a box with papers. Then the shelling recommenced.

"No! No, not again!" she screamed.

"Mother, we have to go," said Miriam. "Any of those shells could land right here."

"I will not leave my house," Mother cried.

It took both girls to pull the distraught woman downstairs. Tiche had already packed the silver in a second pillowcase and gone ahead. The three Morgan women reached the door as four or five shells sailed overhead, making a perfect corkscrew in the air. Mother screamed and as Sarah turned to lock the door, Miriam cried, "Never mind the door!"

With this new music in their ears, they ran to the back gate. Another shell passed so close that Miriam jumped behind the fence for protection.

When it was gone, the trio hurried down one empty street, then another, for everyone else had gone ahead. The shells seemed to be whistling their strange songs for them alone.

The height of my ambition is now attained, thought Sarah. *I have heard Jimmy laugh about the singular sensation produced by the rifled balls spinning around one's head. Now I have heard the same peculiar sound, run the same risk, and am equal to the rest of the boys, for am I not in the midst of flying shells, in the middle of a bombard-ment? I think I am rather proud of it.*

About a mile and a half from home Mother sank to the ground exhausted. It was quieter there, so they rested beside the road until a buggy approached. A gentleman kindly offered to take Mother since he only had room for one passenger.

"I cannot leave you girls," she protested.

"I have a pistol and a dagger, Mother," Sarah told her. "We will be safe enough."

When the gentleman took their bundles as well, Sarah felt as if a great load had been lifted from her shoulders. With fresh confidence, she and Miriam walked on.

Two miles later they caught up with the other fugitives. It was a heartrending scene—girls of twelve and fourteen wandering alone, mothers searching for lost babies, servants caring for those babies or their mistresses' other possessions. Strangers, white and black, suddenly were becoming confidential friends. No one knew if their homes still stood or had been reduced to ashes. Sarah and Miriam were finally invited to ride atop a neighbor's wagonload of goods where a breathless Lucy found them later.

"Lucy! Have you seen Mother and Tiche? Where are Lilly and the children?"

"Up yonder. Mrs. Morgan keeps asking, 'What has become of my poor girls?' So I decide to find you. Miss Lilly is restin' at Mr. David's house."

Despite the misery around her, Sarah felt encouraged and began singing her favorite old hymns, *"Better days are coming,"* and *"I hope to die shouting the Lord will provide."*

Trudging beside the wagon in the sun and dust, Lucy answered with a hearty chorus, *"I'm a runnin', a runnin' up to Glory."*

At three o'clock that afternoon, about six hours after the attack, the Morgans were finally reunited at Seth David's Halfway House. It was a convenient stopover for the many carriages traveling the long, winding Greenwell Springs Road. Today it was crowded with weary refugees and the hasty meal that was served tasted like a feast.

When they were rested, Miriam, Lilly, and the children found an old cart and moved on. Sarah stayed with her mother and Dellie, intending to join the others the next day. About sunset, Charlie's buggy came flying down the dusty road leading back to Baton Rouge.

"Must you go tonight?" asked Mother.

Charlie nodded. "I want to see what shape the

town is in, and if the fighting will move this way."

"I am going, too," Sarah announced.

Mother's look of shock was followed by an obstinate debate in which Sarah was more determined than amiable. In the end she triumphantly rode away with Charlie, confident that he could take care of her; and if something happened to him, she could take care of herself.

It was past nine o'clock when they reached town. Sarah sighed with relief when she saw that the house still stood, dark and deserted. Lighting the lamps, they examined the rooms. There was a noise upstairs.

Sarah froze as Charlie called, "Who's there?"

"Master Charlie, is that you?" came a drowsy voice.

"Tiche?" called Sarah to the figure peeking down the stairwell.

"Miss Sarah, I thought you was at Greenwell! What you doin' back here?"

"We thought you got to Greenwell ahead of us," said Sarah. "Are you all right? Were you here when they did this?"

Tiche shook her head as they stared at the confusion of overturned chairs and scattered clothes. "When I couldn't find you folks on the road, I just come back home. De shellin' was over and Yankees done been here. Dey shore made a mess, lookin' for food and valuables."

Sarah dashed up to her room. She hardly recognized it. The contents of drawers lay scattered about, laces and ribbons all over the floor. Then she noticed a box of trinkets, which Miriam had sworn to die protecting, sitting on the bolster. Sarah picked it up and laughed. "Now Miriam is safe at Greenwell and here you are, forgotten. When under fire, we change our minds about what is important."

Thinking about what Miriam would say when she saw the box, Sarah finished packing the trunk she had begun to fill that morning. She longed to take her guitar and Miriam's piano, but there was simply no room. It was far into the night when she finished and sank into the cold tub of water Tiche had thoughtfully provided before going back to bed. A change of clothes made her feel like a new being, despite a blister that took all the skin off one heel.

After three hours of battle-filled sleep, Sarah rose with the sun. Breakfast was a piece of bread and a glass of clabber, the only food left in the house. Then her mother arrived with Charlie, who shared the news he had learned. It seemed the trouble had started when a Union ship, the *Kennebec,* had sent men in a rowboat to find a washerwoman to do their laundry. They were fired upon by guerrillas hiding in shanties along the wharf, wounding three of the sailors. Union Adm. David Farragut was so upset that he ordered the shelling. The guerrillas slipped away while the town went into general panic.

"Was anyone killed?" asked Mother.

Charlie nodded sadly. "One woman was killed

and three wounded. Indirectly there were others. We know of two little children who drowned in the escape, and sick people who should never have been moved."

"Well, hurrah for the illustrious Farragut!" cried Sarah. "Woman killer!"

"It seems that some gentlemen saved the town by rowing out to tell the commander that he was only killing women and children. They explained that the city has no control over the guerrillas. Farragut apologized and said he thought it had been evacuated."

"Ridiculous," said Sarah. "He was firing straight up the main streets filled with women and children. How could he not see them?"

"I know," said Charlie. "At any rate, Farragut assured the men that he will not fire again unless attacked. A General Williams has just arrived with more troops to protect 'the lives and property of loyal citizens.'"

"Protect us—from what?"

Charlie paused as if reluctant to bear more bad news. "The guerrillas have threatened to burn the town rather than let Federal troops have it."

Sarah felt her chest tighten. "Like the cotton?" she whispered.

He nodded. "Perhaps we should hope that General Williams does his job well."

It was late that night when the weary group

reached Greenwell. Bonfires were lit in front of the rustic pine cabins, giving them a warm, homey look, but Sarah could only wonder about the home she had left. Loving arms welcomed her and found a mattress on which she could finally sleep. She continued to rest the next day as Miriam returned to town with friends in hopes of saving her piano. They had barely left when word reached Greenwell that no one entering Baton Rouge would be allowed to leave without a pass.

Sarah's mother was alarmed and hurried to catch the girls in their cart. They did not return, and by the next day Sarah, too, grew concerned. She walked by the hotel, packed with women and crying, hungry children. Finding a quiet spot, she sat beneath a towering magnolia and toyed with one of its fallen pods. Below her the Amite River wound drowsily by, and she could almost hear her brothers' laughter as they returned from a day of fishing.

Other trips had been so different. They might have started with swimming, bowling, or a stroll through the pine forest. Mother said the trees were so thick at Greenwell that you had to walk a mile to see the sunset. Someone was always giving a party, and the Fourth of July was especially festive.

Sarah remembered one year when her father had been asked to give a speech marking the occasion. A brass band had played as he mounted the podium looking incredibly dignified. It was a lofty, patriotic speech, for Judge Morgan had dearly loved his country. Sarah's eyes grew misty as she relived the day. There had been feasting and dancing in the ballroom far past her bedtime. She had been twelve then—a shy, but happy child, oblivious to the political rumblings that would soon divide her country and destroy her peaceful existence. How she longed to go back to that time, or forward to the end of this dreadful war—to be anywhere but *here and now.*

Chapter 6

❖

Occupation

June 1, Sunday

From the news brought yesterday, I am more uneasy about Mother and the girls. No one is permitted to leave without a pass, and of these, only such as are separated from their families. All families are prohibited to leave, and [taking] furniture, and other valuables also. Think of being obliged to ask permission to go in and out of our own homes! The Yankees are in a constant state of alarm. Their reason for keeping people in town is that they hope they will not be attacked so long as our own friends remain.

Last night a violent wind storm came up, and Lilly was so alarmed that she moved children, servants and all, into the office for safety; but as I could not quite reconcile myself to sleeping in a room with seventeen people, I walked to Mrs. Brunot's in my nightgown and slept there with Dena.

Sunday night. The girls have just got back, riding in a mule team on top of baggage. Our condition is perfectly desperate. Miriam had an interview with General Williams, which was by no means satisfactory. He gave her a pass to leave, and bring us back, for he says there is no safety here for us; he will restrain his men in town, but once outside, he will neither answer for his men, or the women and children. Any house shut up shall be occupied by soldiers. Five thousand are there now, five more expected. What shall we do?

Sarah paused, rubbing her forehead. Mother was determined that she and Miriam go back to town, despite the threat of yellow fever that usually came in June. No one caught the dread disease out in Greenwell, which was one reason why everyone who could afford a cottage spent summers there. Sarah pulled out her running bag and counted the money she had carefully hidden: seventeen hundred dollars in Confederate notes, worthless in Baton Rouge. She also had three or four dollars in silver that might last two days. In town they could starve. Tucking the money and her journal away, she went to find Miriam. "I am of the opinion that we should send for Mother and make our way into the interior. At least in the Confederacy our money will be worth something, and we can communicate with the boys," Sarah told her.

Miriam shook her head. "Mother wants us together, Sarah. And she still has hopes of saving the house."

"Home is lost beyond all hope of recovery," Sarah argued. "And this is not living. I fear the guerrillas will attack the town tonight; if they do, God help Mother!"

"It may not be so dreadful in town. Did I tell you that General Williams offered me an escort when he learned I was alone. His manner was almost fatherly. I think he must be a good man, Sarah."

Sarah argued no further. It was becoming clear that good and bad existed on both sides of this war. If Miriam were right about General Williams, perhaps Baton Rouge would fare better than New Orleans had under Beast Butler.

By the next day she was persuaded to ride home with the Brunots, perched atop the same mule wagon. A blistering sun followed them along the dusty road, past guerrilla picket lines. The makeshift soldiers warned against returning to Baton Rouge, but the wagon rolled on.

"Miss Sarah ain't ashamed to ride in a wagon," remarked one of the servants.

Sarah imagined how odd she and Nettie Brunot must look, dignified Southern ladies bouncing along on the baggage. "No, I never was so high before," she laughed.

Passing by the graveyard at the edge of the city, Sarah noticed how the Yankee camp had grown in population. Men and cannon were everywhere. Instead of warnings, here the wagon was met with loud laughter. Sarah dropped her veil, for it was all she could do not to smile back.

Finally the wagon lumbered onto Church Street. A group of officers standing near the Morgan house chuckled as they pulled up. Suddenly Sarah didn't feel like smiling any longer. *After reducing us to riding in a mule team, how heartless they are to laugh,* she thought. Then her attention was turned to a new problem—how to get down respectably.

It was a three-foot drop to the wheel. Once there, the driver lifted her down. Holding on to him, Sarah felt her hairnet slip and her long hair tumble to full length below her knees. Trying to ignore the eyes that bore into her and maintain some dignity, she grabbed her bundle from the wagon and started for the house. She recalled having read once that queens in olden days sometimes rode in wagons drawn by oxen. So she imagined that she were a queen and the mules were oxen, then stalked off with a style that would have impressed Queen Juno herself. *A lady can make anything respectable by the way she does it, Sarah decided.*

Once indoors, "Queen" Sarah was relieved to find her mother was safe, although the house was in total disarray. Jimmy's empty bird cage still stood by the door. The sight of it stabbed her heart as she wondered what had become of her little friend. She became aware of hunger gnawing at her stomach. "Mother, is there anything to eat?"

Mother shook her head sadly as she rummaged through boxes. Sarah tried to help, but found herself counting the hours since her last meal, a bite of hoecake. Twelve hours—she had never been good at fasting. She and Miriam had tried it last Ash Wednesday and had grown so queasy that they atoned by dinnertime.

Was there any place to buy food? Sarah went next door to find out. Along with advice, Mrs. Daigre offered what she had, bread and corned beef. Hearing of the Morgans' plight, another friend later brought short cake and strawberry preserves. Sarah was grateful and ate sparingly, realizing that the old Negro woman was sharing her own supper. "Eat it all, honey!" she insisted. "I got plenty more."

The next day Sarah ventured out, hoping to find provisions of her own. Another family friend, Dr. Castleton, escorted her part of the way. She appreciated the company, for the streets of Baton Rouge had been transformed. Yankees were everywhere. Some played cards in the dry ditch by the roadside, swearing dreadfully. Some marched, while some slept on the pavement and others picked odious bugs from each other's hair. Sarah thought of the guerrillas camped in the woods fighting yellow fever as well, and wished that all could be safe at home with their mothers and sisters. Finally, she returned home alone, trying not to cringe as she passed through a large group of soldiers.

It was late when Sarah pulled out her worn little journal. She held it gently between her palms, thankful that it had not been lost in the flight to Greenwell, and spoke softly: "If you are not captured and burned for treason, and I live through this, I might like to read you one of these days." Then she took a pen and, yawning, began to write. There was so much to record about the past three days. Sarah wished that she were not so tired.

Baton Rouge June 3d.

What a day I have had! Here mother and I are alone, not a servant on the lot. We will sleep here tonight, and I know she will be too nervous to let me sleep. The dirt and confusion was extraordinary in the house. I could not stand it, so I applied myself to making it better. I actually swept two whole rooms! I ruined my hands at gardening, so it made no difference. I replaced piles of books, crockery, china, that Miriam had left packed for Greenwell; I discovered I could empty a dirty hearth, dust, move heavy weights, make myself generally useful and dirty, and all this is thanks to the Yankees!

Chapter 7

——— ❖ ———

Mr. Biddle

Sarah felt a thousand years old. Rumors of a large Confederate force coming to reclaim Baton Rouge had everyone disturbed. Troops passed constantly and Mother was in a frenzy—should they stay and protect the house from vandals or face starvation at Greenwell? Miriam had returned home, and after long discussion, was sent to General Williams with the keys to the house. Mother hoped that it would be safer left at his disposal.

When Miriam returned, Sarah met her in the yard. "Did you see the General? What did he say?"

Miriam hurried in, closing the door to the dust from the street. "I told him our situation, but he already seemed to know all about us. He even called me by name and asked about Major Drum."

"How would he know about our brother-in-law?"

"I have no idea, but perhaps the General is more considerate because the Major is on their side. At any rate, he will send a sentinel to protect the house so that we may leave."

Sarah was speechless for a moment. "I suppose Mother will be relieved to hear that," she said finally.

Before they had the chance to tell her, there was a knock at the door. Expecting a neighbor, Sarah was taken aback by the blue uniform. A trim fellow, somewhat older than herself, removed his hat. "Miss Morgan?"

"Yes."

"Lt. James Biddle, ma'am. Aide to General Williams. He sent me to discuss the matter of posting a sentinel."

"Oh," was all Sarah could think to say.

"Who is it?" Mother called.

"Mr. Biddle, from General Williams," Sarah called back. Then her eyes brightened. "I recognize your name from the passes. We have requested so many, you must think we are all insane."

The man named Biddle almost smiled as he shook his head. "Not at all. These are very perplexing times." He paused, turning the dark hat between his hands.

Sarah knew that by all rules of propriety it was her turn to speak, to invite the visitor to come in, sit, and speak his peace. Yet she felt as if all eyes on Church Street were riveted to the Yankee on her doorstep. What would the neighbors think? What should she do?

Biddle cleared his throat and spoke in a low, earnest voice. "Miss Morgan, the General wished me to speak with your mother, if she is available."

Sarah drew a deep breath. "Mr. Biddle, would you like to come in?"

After a long discussion on their home's need for protection, Mr. Biddle left. "All tongues in Baton Rouge will be flapping now," Sarah commented. "But I do not regret asking him in."

"You did the right thing, Sarah," her mother said. "Mr. Biddle is certainly a gentleman and honest enough to admit there are bad characters among their soldiers who would rob a home left vacant."

"All true, but having Federal soldiers guarding the place may cause more than tongues to wag," Miriam warned. "We will be labeled as traitors. If our forces take the town back, they will surely confiscate the house."

For a long, silent moment Mother held her face in her hands. Making important decisions was a new experience for her since Father had died. Doing so under such frightening circumstances was nearly an unbearable ordeal. Finally, she spoke in a tight, weary voice. "Our other alternative is to stay here. Then a sentinel will be not necessary."

Sarah and Miriam nodded in agreement. For now they would stay. When the sentinels came at dusk, Miriam met them in the yard. It took some time to convince the officer in charge, a Colonel McMillan, that their presence was unnecessary. Sarah was struck by the irony of the situation. *Here our brothers are off fighting Federals while this man stands on our doorstep offering to protect us, she thought. What a strange war.*

Two evenings later, the Morgan ladies were invited to supper at the Brunots. It was a simple meal compared to those in days past, but any food was precious and appreciated. The June day was long, so there were two full hours of light left to sit on the gallery. A breeze from the river cooled their faces and soothed ruffled nerves. Yet far down the street heavy footsteps could be heard marching in unison. A Yankee commander barked orders to his troops as they came into view, and conversation on the porch dropped to whispers. Then the soldiers stopped directly in front of the Brunot house, where they turned to face the women.

There was no sound as each stared at the other. Sarah tried to ignore the soldiers by looking up at the sky, but that seemed ridiculous. So she faced them, from the lowly privates to a smiling, red-headed lieutenant. Yet as the moments passed, she wished desperately for them to move on. Five minutes dragged by.

Finally, when she was on the brink of crying with embarrassment, the order was given for the men to drill. They were well practiced and drilled splendidly, not at all like soldiers who had already marched an hour in the heat. Sarah noticed that the red-headed lieutenant continued to smile as if quite pleased with the impression he was making.

When it was over and the street was quiet again, Sarah walked home with Mother and Miriam. They were sitting in the moonlight on their own balcony when Mr. Biddle arrived. With hardly a second thought, Sarah ushered him in.

He bowed, courteously as before. "Good evening, Mrs. Morgan. General Williams sends his regards and wishes to know if the sentinel came as instructed."

When Mother explained about their change in plans, Mr. Biddle did not seem surprised. It occurred to Sarah that he could have saved himself the walk by asking Colonel McMillan himself. Yet as the next two hours passed, she found Mr. Biddle to be an entertaining guest. His news of the war seemed more sensible than the abusive newspapers that screamed headlines from their own patriotic viewpoints. She tried not to notice the stares of people passing by, both citizens and soldiers, shocked by the Morgans and their guest obviously enjoying themselves.

"I understand that flour, among other things, is growing scarce in town," Mr. Biddle observed. "We have a good supply at the garrison. Would you permit me to send a barrel over?"

Sarah's eyes widened as she and Miriam looked at Mother. Hospitality was one thing, but to be *fed* by the Yankees . . .

"I appreciate your concern, sir, but we must decline," said Mother.

Sarah breathed a sigh of relief, imagining what the town would have said about *that*.

The flour came anyway.

"These people mean to kill us with kindness," Sarah declared.

Mother opened the note accompanying the barrel of flour General Williams had sent. "He begs us to accept it in consideration of present conditions," she read. "I suppose it would be rude to return it, but I wish he had not. Sarah, please write him a note of thanks."

"Mother, no! I have never written to a stranger before. Miriam knows him—let her do it."

"Miriam is busy and you can be quite eloquent, Sarah. Anyone who spends as much time with her diary as you do should not object to writing a simple thank you note."

Sarah grumbled all the way to her room. After several false starts she composed three lines that did not sound terribly foolish.

The next morning she was glad she had written the note. As Sarah's family stood waiting for the church door to be opened for services, a large group of officers arrived. Miriam tugged on Sarah's sleeve and nodded toward a trim, bearded man. "That's General Williams," she whispered.

Sarah watched as they came closer. No one spoke of flour or sentinels, but General Williams recognized Miriam and bowed deeply to the Morgan ladies. Sarah could feel the cold stares of neighbors as they curtsied in return. Then everyone filed into the church.

By tomorrow, those he did not bow to will cry treason against us, she thought. *Let them howl. I am tired of lies, scandal and deceit. All the loudest gossips have been frightened into the country, but enough remain to keep them well supplied with town talk. I wish people would find some family equally worthy of their attention, besides ours.*

Chapter 8

❖

Between Two Fires

Tuesday dawned bright and dew-sparkled. As was her custom, Sarah rose before seven o'clock and took advantage of the cool morning breeze to work in her garden. It consisted of two rows running the length of the house where flowers were often uprooted by a passing horse or cow. Hoeing energetically, she was startled by a flash of pale yellow wings that landed on her shoulder and chirped.

"Jimmy!" she cried. "Where did you come from?"

Sarah slowly reached for the tiny bird, noticing how dingy his once-bright feathers had become. "It's good to have you home."

But as her hand approached, Jimmy fluttered away.

"Wait," she pleaded. "You are so dirty. I'm sure I can better care of you than you are taking of yourself." Then her shoulders slumped as Jimmy vanished into the trees. "Oh, come back, Birdy. I must have something to pet."

However, it appeared that Jimmy had only stopped to say "hello." Sarah turned sadly to her geraniums, hardly noticing the soldiers striding down the pavement. They stopped in front of her, hanging over the fence like schoolboys.

"Good morning, miss."

Sarah nodded, wishing they would go away.

"You have a lovely garden," said one soldier in a brisk New England accent.

"Thank you."

"Did you hear the excitement last night?"

"No," said Sarah, sure that she was about to be told.

"Colonel McMillan got shot up in a skirmish with guerrillas. They brought him to the hospital right across the street there," the soldier said, pointing to a three-story brick building on the corner.

Sarah recognized the name of the officer who had come to guard the house. "McMillan, did you say?"

"Yes, ma'am. And he is one tough fellow, let me tell you."

Curiosity got the best of her. "Why? What happened?" she asked.

"He was on a scout a few miles from town and got shot by guerrillas. They say he killed the fellow who shot him, and brought in two prisoners. Was shot three times, but didn't fall off his horse 'til he got to camp!"

"My goodness," said Sarah. "Will he live?"

"Don't know."

"Do you know who the prisoners are—what has happened to them?"

The soldier shook his head and rambled on

about Colonel McMillan's bravery and other Yankee exploits. Sarah decided that he would talk as long as she listened, and went back to her work. When the group finally moved on, she hurried in to tell Mother and Miriam of Colonel McMillan's misfortune.

"I had heard they were using part of the Heroman building as a hospital," said Miriam.

"Colonel McMillan was so sincere in offering to protect us," said Sarah. "I wish we could do something for him."

Mother frowned thoughtfully. "It is our Christian duty to help those in need, no matter what uniform they wear."

Sarah's eyes met her mother's. "He was shot three times. Surely he must be in desperate need."

"Bandages," said Mother. "And something nourishing. With only men managing things, there is no telling what they eat in that makeshift hospital."

"But we have so little to cook," Sarah reminded her.

"We have flour. Tiche can come up with something."

"Wait!" Miriam protested. "What will people say? We are already under suspicion as traitors for allowing Mr. Biddle in. Visiting the Yankee hospital will remove all doubt."

"We have a higher duty than appeasing public opinion," argued Sarah. "Do unto others as you would they should do unto you, remember?"

Miriam stood. "Defying public opinion could

cost us dearly," she said. "I did not want to mention it, but a lady told me yesterday that the guerrillas have a black list of those believed to be traitors. The men are to be hanged, their houses burned, and the women tarred and feathered."

"Another rumor," argued Sarah. "I do not believe our own men are such brutes."

"Is this Yankee colonel worth taking that chance?"

Mother's pale face was resolute. The girls hushed, knowing the final decision was hers. "One's religion is worth little if abandoned during times of trial. We will send what we have in the hope it might offer the colonel some comfort. Sarah, there is linen packed in one of those trunks that can be used for bandages. I will speak to Tiche about preparing food. It will draw less attention if she delivers it as well."

Sarah nodded in agreement and Miriam stalked from the room. As she searched for the linen, Sarah pondered over the effects the war was having on the characters of people. Miriam had always been brave, noble, generous. The strain of being caught between two fires, Christian conscience and public opinion, was wearing her down. Then there were the real fires of Yankee gunboats in front and their own forces behind.

Our three brothers may be sick or wounded at this minute, thought Sarah. *What I do for this man, God will send someone to do for them. Let our "friends" burn our home for it. I would be proud to sacrifice myself for God and Religion. Mob shall never govern my opinions, or tell me how much I may be allowed to do. I will do what Conscience alone dictates.*

The next morning found the Morgans visiting the Arsenal to see if they could do anything for the two Confederate prisoners Colonel McMillan had brought in. Both boys, Nathan Castle and Willie Garig, were sons of respected local families. They appreciated the ladies' visit and said their only need was for clean clothes. Sarah spent the afternoon mending some of her brothers' suits that might fit them. Later, Tiche delivered the clothes in a magnificent bundle wrapped Creole style around her head. Hearing that Mr. Biddle was sick, Sarah sent a custard as well.

"We can do more than this," she told Mother as they watched Tiche gracefully cross the street with her bundle. "They say that more than a hundred Federal soldiers lie sick in the new theater. Could we not minister to some of them as well?"

"We could be ostracized just for helping those two men who have done us a kindness," Mother reminded her.

"Are we too patriotic to refuse a dying man a drink of cold water? To write letters and offer comfort? What if George or Gibbes or Jimmy lay in some Northern hospital with no one to attend them? I would hope that some Northern woman would forget her patriotism in the name of compassion."

"Sarah, that's enough," Mother commanded sharply. "Please do not insist on bringing the town's wrath down upon us."

Biting her tongue, Sarah ran upstairs, where she spent the next hour with her diary. It was her release, a lightning rod for her mental thunder on these impossible days. Words that might burn and wound another soul could strike safely here. Counting the few pages left in her journal, she wondered how she would survive when it was full and there was no other place to vent her frustrations.

The long summer days stretched into another week. A lack of food at Greenwell forced Lilly's family back to town and returned the house to a livelier routine. After breakfast and gardening, Sarah acted as teacher for Lilly's two oldest children before turning to her own studies. Except for ten months of formal schooling, she had been educated at home, but an insatiable thirst for learning had led her to continue on her own. Some days she marveled at the mysteries of arithmetic and geography, and on others would lose herself in French grammar and literature. Time before and after dinner was spent writing and sewing.

Somewhere in the day, Sarah would find half an hour to spend at the piano, for both she and Miriam loved music. At twilight it was their custom to sit on the balcony and sing with the guitar. Afterward came reading until the house quieted down about ten o'clock. When the younger servants' chores were finished, they would gather in Sarah's room for Bible class. She would first read or tell a story, after which Lucy, Rose, Nancy, and Dophy would take turns saying their prayers. Their grievances from the day were usually aired at this time, and Sarah often felt like Moses trying to judge the Israelites.

On one particular night, Sarah had tried to persuade quick-tempered Rose to apologize for stabbing Lucy's arm with a fork. Rose finally repented and surprised all with flood of tears. It seemed that Dophy had wronged Lucy as well, so a touching scene of kissing and reconciliation followed. Sarah was amazed by Lucy's forgiving nature and buoyant spirit as the girl began to sing. When the hymn was done, they went off to bed with, "Good night, Miss Sarah," and "God bless Miss Sarah."

Ah me, thought Sarah, *children and servants like me even if big people don't. I believe I prefer it.*

June 16th Monday

My poor old diary comes to a very abrupt end, to my great distress. The hardest thing in the world is to break off journalizing when you are one accustomed to it. Mine has proved such a resource to me in these dark days of trouble that I feel as though I were saying goodbye to an old and tried friend.

Chapter 9

❖

The Beast

"I hope to die shouting the Lord will provide," Sarah sang as she bounded down the attic stairs clutching the small book she had found there. It was an old ledger of her father, not a true diary, but clean and inviting to her pen:

Monday June 16th, 1862.

There is no use in trying to break off journalizing, particularly in "these trying times." It has become a necessity to me. I get nervous and unhappy in thinking of the sad condition of the country and of the misery in store for us; get desperate to think I am fit for nothing in the world, could not earn my daily bread even. Just before I reach the lowest ebb, I dash off half a dozen lines, sing "Better days are coming" and Presto! am myself again.

But today I am weary of everything. I wish I could find some lodge in some vast wilderness where I could be in peace and quiet; where I would never hear of war, or rumors of war, of lying, slandering, and all uncharitableness; where I could eat my bread in thanksgiving and trust God alone in all things; a place where I would never hear a woman talk politics. What a consolation it is to remember there are no "Politics" in heaven!

In my opinion the Southern women have disgraced themselves by their rude, ill mannered behavior. Lieutenant Biddle assured me he did not pass a street in New Orleans without being most grossly insulted by ladies. It was a friend of his into whose face a lady spit as he walked quietly by without looking at her. He had the sense to apply to her husband and give him two minutes to apologize or die, and of course he chose the former.

This war has brought out wicked malignant feelings that I did not believe could dwell in a woman's heart. I see some go off in a mad tirade and say, "I hope God will send down plague, Yellow fever, famine, on these vile Yankees, and that not one will escape death."

Oh, what unutterable horror that remark causes me! I think of the many mothers, wives and sisters who wait as anxiously, pray as fervently in their far away lonesome homes for their dear ones, as we do here. I fancy them waiting day after day for the footsteps that will never come. I think of how awful it would be to me if one would say "your brothers are dead," how it would crush all the life and happiness out of me; and I say, "God forgive these poor women! They know not what they say!"

As the week passed the river bustled with boats transporting troops upriver to Vicksburg. The city on the bluffs was still defended by Confederate forces and remained a major obstacle to Union control of the Mississippi. General Williams was sent to command what was rumored to be the digging of a canal to divert the river there. Sarah was sorry to see him go, fearing what new leadership might bring.

On June 28th she found out. It began with cannon fire that brought frightened women, children, and servants to their front porches. Had another bombardment begun? Despite the crying of her nieces and nephews, Sarah could hear her heart pounding as they waited for news. *What was happening?*

Then the word came. The shots were not the start of another bombardment, but a salute to honor the new commander—Gen. Benjamin Butler. The Beast had arrived.

"How coolly Butler will grind them down, paying no regard to their writhing and torture beyond tightening the bands still more," Sarah read from the newspaper. "He is the right man in the right place. He will develop a Union sentiment among the people, if the thing can be done." She lowered the paper, her cheeks flushed and blue eyes ablaze. "The man is a tyrant!"

Miriam nodded as she knitted. "Mother and I saw that in New Orleans. At least we will no longer be considered traitors, for I doubt that General Butler will send flour. Does it say anything about the men he imprisoned?"

Sarah shook her head. "They say Mr. Craven, the Methodist minister, was arrested for praying for the Confederacy with his family in his own house. If that is a crime, they might as well arrest us all. Show me the dungeon deep enough to keep me from praying from my brothers."

Mother rocked nervously. "By arresting community leaders they set an example. But how do they know what goes on in private homes?"

"Detectives," Sarah told her. "It says here that a man has been assigned to watch every house. And listen to this about foreign intervention on our behalf: 'Butler says that if France or England interferes, he will arm every negro in the south with orders to cut the throat of every man, woman and child in it!'"

Mother shuddered as Sarah paced about the room. "This is supposed to create Union sentiment?" she fumed at the small portrait above the newspaper column. General Butler's heavy-lidded eyes and square, balding head reminded her of a bulldog; apparently he shared the breed's propensity for blood as well. "Draw me a finer portrait of Coward, Brute, and Bully than this!"

The fly buzzed Sarah again. Folding the paper, she watched it land on the parlor table. Taking careful aim, she swatted hard, making the old lamp dance precariously. Mother grabbed it as Sarah examined her prey—a black smudge. "Oh, if only I were a man and could so deal with you, Mr. Butler."

"We cannot stay," said Mother. "With Butler here

and our own forces coming to reclaim Baton Rouge, perhaps we would be safer with your brother in New Orleans. He has written asking us to come."

"I cannot see where New Orleans would be an improvement," Sarah argued. "Besides, there have been so many rumors. Who knows if General Beauregard truly is marching here?"

"We will wait and be certain," said Mother, "but have your things ready, just in case."

Remembering the mad run to Greenwell, Sarah once again organized her necessaries and wondered how to best carry them. Buggies and trunks could not be counted on in an emergency. The knapsacks worn by schoolboys and soldiers had always looked practical, but since they were not considered ladies' wear, Sarah had never owned one. After some trial and error, she and Miriam devised two sturdy sacks by sewing strong black bands to pillowcases.

When they were finished, Sarah slipped her arms through the straps and smiled at her reflection in the mirror. "What a charming improvement to our pillowcases," she said. "I look like an old peddler."

"And hopefully can carry as much," said Miriam.

Once again Sarah packed her treasures—the prayer book, diaries, pens, daguerreotypes of people she loved. Fortunately there was more room for clothes this time. Her old running bag was filled with toiletries and a dress was carefully spread on the chair in case of alarm when she retired late that night. "I'll lay me down and sleep in peace, for thou only Lord makest me to dwell in safety," she told Miriam, quoting the Fourth Psalm. "Good night! I believe we will wake up tomorrow as usual and be disappointed that all this trouble was unnecessary."

Sarah was right. The next day, July 4th, came and went without incident. With the arrest of a local newspaper editor, papers ceased, and news consisted of rumors. Their minister, Mr. Gierlow, left for Europe. Without Sunday service the day seemed like any other. It was ten o'clock that night when Sarah went up to bed, leaving Mother to talk with a neighbor through the window. Then her quick footsteps were heard on the stairs. "Charlie! Come quickly! There is a man in the alley!"

Sarah dashed to her window and strained to see through the darkness. A man crouched in the shadow of the fence beneath the window. Sarah watched quietly, wondering what he would do next. When Charlie's heavy steps were heard, the man ran to the front of the house. It was a noisy escape through the tangle of long, dried grass that had grown up in the alley. Upon reaching the corner of the house, he paused, straightened up to full height, and walked toward the front gate. In the moonlight Sarah could see that he wore a neat black suit and gave the appearance of a gentleman.

"You there!" Charlie called from the upstairs gallery. "State your business!"

Without answering, the man closed the gate,

then suddenly lurched as if he were drunk and disappeared down the street.

The family met downstairs and tried to calm Mother. "That man was spying on us!" she cried.

"Well, he heard no treason this night," said Sarah. "But imagine pretending to be drunk. We are not such fools."

The Morgans did not see the black-suited eavesdropper again. Sarah felt as if she were living on a volcano as one day blurred into another. However, as the shock of being spied upon was forgotten, the girls returned to their routine of music on the balcony. Only Charlie protested that they were attracting unnecessary attention, but how could he understand? Some of their fondest memories were of entertaining Father with an evening concert.

So the music continued, with Miriam playing guitar as she joined Sarah in their favorite old songs. It was easy to ignore the soldiers passing below for they appeared to be minding their own affairs and must certainly know the girls were not singing for *their* benefit. Then one night, after the last notes of "Mary of Argyle," came a burst of applause.

Sarah froze in horror. Miriam silenced the guitar strings as Charlie cried, "I told you so!" and everyone rushed inside. In a matter of seconds, the balcony was empty.

As Mother closed windows and turned off the gaslights, Sarah and Miriam flew upstairs. They had to know who their audience was. Creeping out onto the dark upper balcony, they now became the spies. In the moonlit yard next door a man stood beneath a tree. His hands were thrust deep in his pockets as he watched the windows of the Morgan house darken. Unlike the spy in the alley, there was nothing sinister about this forlorn fellow.

"He looks as though he'd been kicked," whispered Sarah.

"There's another one!" Miriam pointed as the shadows stirred and another man stood. His hands sought his pockets, too, and if possible, he seemed more mortified than the first.

"I suppose they were just enjoying our music and meant no harm," said Sarah.

"I wonder what uncivilized place they come from to have acquired such manners," whispered Miriam.

The men watched the dark house awhile as if hoping the music might resume. Finally realizing that they had put an end to future singing on the balcony, they slowly walked away. Something tugged at Sarah's heart as the two looked back every few steps, just to be sure.

"Perhaps their mothers sang the same old songs when they were babies, and it reminded them of home," she said wistfully. "Oh Yankees, why did you do such a thoughtless thing?"

Chapter 10

❖

Asylum

July 11th

A letter from George this morning! It was written on the 20th [of] June, and he speaks of being on crutches, in consequence of his horse having fallen with him, and injured his knee. Jimmy is with him at Richmond. Gibbes he had heard from in a letter dated the sixteenth, and up to then he was in perfect health.

July 12th

I grow desperate when I read these Northern papers reviling and abusing us, taunting us with their victories, sparing no humiliating name when speaking of us; that seem written expressly to goad us into madness! There must be many humane, reasonable men in the North; can they not teach their Editors decency in this their hour of triumph?

July 13th, Sunday.

This evening the mosquitoes are so savage that writing became impossible, until Miriam and I instituted a grand Extermination process. She lay on the bed with the bar half drawn over her, and half

*looped up, while I was commissioned to fan the
wretches from all corners in to the pen. It was rather
fatiguing, and in spite of the number slain, hardly
recompensed me for the trouble; but still Miriam
says exercise is good for me, and she ought to know.*

July 17, Thursday.

*Everything points to an early attack here. The
Federals are cutting down our beautiful woods to
throw up breastworks. I was so distressed this
evening! They tell me Mr. Biddle was killed at
Vicksburg. I hope it is not true. Suppose it was a
shot from Will's battery?*

It was Sunday again. Sarah stood alone on the
front balcony watching the activity about St. James
church down the street. In preparation for the
coming attack, a Yankee force had camped there,
and instead of worshippers gathering for service,
tents had popped up like toadstools in front of the
church. On the commons behind it stood cannon
and artillery horses.

She yawned and rubbed weary red eyes. A false
alarm at midnight had caused total confusion both
in her house and the streets. No one knew what to
expect anymore. Even the dispatches coming from
Confederate forts upriver were contradictory:
"Forts have been taken . . . Yankees at our mercy
. . . City under British protection . . . No it isn't . .
. City surrendered . . . Mistake . . . Baton Rouge to
be burned when Yankee ships come . . ."

Miriam, also yawning, joined her. "Charlie says that

he will take Lilly and the children to the country tomorrow."

"Good," said Sarah. "Then I can take whatever comes. This constant alarm with five babies in the house is just too much."

The hours passed quickly with all hands helping to pack Lilly's brood. Then as the hot July day melted into evening a drum roll was heard down the street. It was followed by the pounding of hooves and shouting. "Only eight miles . . . ten thousand of 'em!" was all Sarah could make out. Was it another false alarm, or was the battle about to begin?

"To the Asylum," shouted Charlie.

As Beatrice and Louis wailed, Dellie tugged at her father's coat. "Why are we going there? Isn't that for deaf and blind people?"

Charlie scooped her into his arms. "Tonight it is a safe place for everyone. The director has invited all of you."

Though the children were already packed, it took an hour for the Morgans to join the confusion in the street. Sarah counted seventeen of her household, white and black, each loaded in his or her own way. Outside the heat was stifling as wagons, carts, and every vehicle imaginable sought safety. It was many squares to the State Asylum for the Deaf and Blind on the southern edge of Baton Rouge, yet Sarah didn't mind the walk. After the tension of waiting, she almost felt merry.

The five-story building was an impressive Gothic

structure, fully lit like a grand hotel. Inside Sarah was surprised to see none of the residents since the first floor had been cleared for the refugees. While Lilly and the children settled down in one room, Sarah, Miriam, and the Brunot sisters romped in the halls. It became a fine game to dash down the long corridors amid a gauntlet of pillows and clothing. Their laughter and squeals finally brought Sarah's mother and Mrs. Brunot out to cry "Order!" However, the roughhousing was a welcome relief from the tension, and soon the mothers were part of the game.

It was late before the house grew quiet as exhausted women and children slumbered. Sarah's bed consisted of a hard little mattress on the floor without a mosquito bar. Her bare arms were no defense against the buzzing tormentors, and the night was much too warm for a blanket. As she tossed and swatted, a racket began upstairs. Apparently someone thought they had heard cannon fire and everyone on that floor stampeded to their balcony. Sarah lay still, determined not to believe it, and eventually all grew quiet again.

Then the door opened. "Sarah, Miriam, are you awake?" came a soft whisper. It was Nettie Brunot.

"I certainly am," Sarah whispered back.

"We are going out on the balcony where it's cooler."

"I will be right there," said Sarah. Throwing on her blue muslin dress and a cape, she joined Nettie and Dena Brunot. Outside they found a splendid breeze whipping around the northwest corner of the building, cooling their faces and relieving the mosquito problem. Settling there, they talked for hours, about nearly everything except the War—books, characters, authors, travel—and men, of course.

"Well, marriage is awful I am sure, but to be an old maid is more awful still," said twenty-year-old Dena.

"I disagree," declared Sarah. "If I had my choice of wretchedness on either hand, I would take it alone; for then I only would be to blame. I will probably be an old maid, for I can fancy no greater punishment than to be tied to a man you could not respect and love perfectly."

"And what sort of man would that be?"

Leaning her elbows on the rail, Sarah cupped her chin in her hands and thought a moment. "Well, my lord and master must be someone I shall never have to blush for; the one that after God, I shall most respect. And as I cannot respect a fool, he must be intelligent. I consider it the chief qualification in a man, just as a pure heart is the chief beauty of a woman."

"All right, he must be smart," agreed Nettie. "Then handsome, yes?"

"He may be as ugly as mud," Sarah declared. "Who ever saw a perfect face on man or woman that showed a spark of intellect? Handsome men seem to care much more for their beauty than their morals. No, he must be amiable. I could be forever cheerful where I had a kind heart to meet mine and make me laugh."

"I agree with that," said Nettie. "What else?"

"He must be as brave as man can be," said Sarah. "I am no coward—it does not run in our blood, so how could I respect a man who was?"

"I think I have met a few who meet your qualifications," said Dena.

"Well, I have not," said Sarah. "At least not in Baton Rouge. Perhaps there is one somewhere. That's it! He is Somewhere Else, for he must be a man of the world. I have seen so little of it that I would wish to be with a gentleman who has."

"It sounds like he must be rich as well," said Nettie.

"Born into a respectable family, yes, but a man need not be wealthy to be a gentleman. That comes from a sense of honor and generous heart. And he must have a profession. If a man is willing and able to work, he can bear whatever fortune brings."

"My word, Sarah, you are particular," Dena teased. "Cupid's arrow may have difficulty penetrating your armor of lofty ideals."

"Good! If I ever meet such a man I will tumble heels over head in love and get married forthwith, even if I have to do the courting. Until then, Cupid, spare my heart! I will need it all for him and am inclined to believe that hearts and eggs are the same—they keep fresh if you let them alone, but get woefully addled by being tossed about!"

The night dragged on endlessly. Conversation drifted and finally Nettie retired. "I believe we shall have no leap year in '64, for the extra twenty-four hours are being crowded in this night," Sarah told Dena.

"The sun is not doing his usual duty," her friend agreed.

In the dim starlight they wandered around the balconies and across the Asylum grounds until the cloudy sky began to show promise of morning. Inside the refugees stirred to get ready for the walk home. Thankfully, there was no damage. After Lilly and the children were seen off to Greenwell, Sarah was finally able to sleep.

The next night another alarm came, meaning a second trip to the Asylum under threatening skies. This time Sarah was given a baby mattress and shared a mosquito bar with Miriam. She slept little and again there was no attack.

On Sunday Sarah was surprised by a knock on the door and a loud "chirp." Lucy Daigre from next door appeared, holding a small brass cage. "Hello, Lucy, what is this? Why, it's Jimmy!"

"He was in our yard after the shelling. I am sorry for not bringing him back sooner."

"Then some other bird must have perched on my shoulder that day," Sarah observed, taking her little friend. "Well, thank you for bringing him back now when we need some cheer. It saddens me to even look out the window. I have never seen so many sick and injured men as are being carried by today."

"We heard that General Williams is back," Lucy told her.

Sarah nodded. "They say the canal they tried to dig at Vicksburg was a fiasco. Imagine trying to turn the Mississippi River. I thought General Williams was a wiser man, but perhaps he was just following orders. Anyway, the men were dropping like flies from heat, malaria, and other ailments. Now Baton Rouge has become one enormous hospital."

"Mr. Baumstark is staying busy. He and his assistants can't make coffins fast enough," Lucy said with a shudder.

Sarah sadly shook her head.

Four days later a note came from Charlie: *"Breckenridge advancing on the Greenwell Springs Road with 10,000 men. Could arrive by tomorrow evening. Leave today! Tell no one as it might warn the Federals. Just go."*

"To leave our home again," Mother moaned.

"This is no false alarm. Charlie went to a good deal of trouble to warn us," said Miriam.

"Phillie Nolan has written to offer us sanctuary at her father's plantation. We should be safe on the other side of the river," said Sarah.

"We will need a pass to cross," Miriam reminded them.

"Do you think you can secure a pass?" Mother asked.

"Of course. They are only twenty-five cents now. Apparently the Yankees need the money."

"Very well. Send Phillie a note, Sarah. We shall leave for Port Allen as soon as possible."

Sarah was heading for the door when Miriam reminded her, "Remember to tell no one about the attack. We are just leaving town as others have done, and all have been warned to do."

The chilling reality of those words sank in. "But what about the Brunots, the Daigres, and our other friends? They may wait until there is no escape."

Holding her face in her hands, Mother moaned again. Sarah wished she would stop. "All right, Sarah, tell the Brunots! Like us, they have no protector. But you must swear them to secrecy."

"Yes, Mother," Sarah cried as she ran out the door.

Chapter 11

❖

The Battle of Baton Rouge

Monday, August 4th. 1862. Westover.

A fresh volume! Where shall I be at the end of it? Will I be once more seated at my old desk in my little room, comfortably settled at home? Or will I have no home then? Will the blank pages record the burning of Baton Rouge, and the loss of our all? Will the close of it find me still running, or at last settled in what is to be our future dwelling in New Orleans? Will they leave us at Peace, or in war? Wait patiently, I say. This war cannot last forever; and then comes blessed Peace!

Here we are at Dr. Nolan's plantation, with Baton Rouge lying just seven miles from us to the east. We can surely hear the cannon from here. They are all so kind to us, that I ought to be contented; but still I wish I was once more at home. I miss my old desk very much; it is so awkward to write on my knee that I cannot get used to it. Mine is a nice little room up stairs, detached from all the rest, for it is formed by a large dormer window looking to the north, from which I have seen a large number of guerrillas passing and repassing

*in their rough costumes. Ginnie Nolan and
Miriam are already equipped in their riding costumes, so I must lay this down, and get ready to
join them in a scamper across the fields. How
delighted I will be to get on a horse again.*

Their ride was so delightful that the girls were up
early the next day, anxious to enjoy another in the
cool of the morning. The sky across the river was
streaked with pink as they galloped along the grassy
levee built to hold the Mississippi within its banks. Its
muddy waters slid lazily by, oblivious to the blood
and toil of men fighting to control its great highway.

Despite the warnings of impending battle, the
river was quiet and their ride without incident until
they returned to the plantation. As Sarah tried to
dismount, her stepladder fell, throwing her hard to
the ground. She was shaken, but still enjoyed a
hearty late breakfast. They were just finishing
when a rapid knock brought everyone outside. It
was one of the guerrillas.

"Just thought you folks would like to know, the
Arkansas is lying just a few miles below on its way
to help General Breckenridge. We expect he's trying to pin the Yanks against the river and let the
Arkansas do the rest."

"You mean our forces have finally attacked
Baton Rouge?"

The fellow nodded vigorously. "Started before
daylight. The advance guard has already driven
the pickets into town."

The group went wild. "Hurrah for Breckenridge!

He'll send those Yankees packing yet! May the Good Lord help our boys.

In the distance, the loud report of half a dozen cannon was heard. "We must see this," the girls squealed as they headed for the barn.

"Miriam, Sarah, no! Come back this instant!" Mother yelled.

Her warning fell on deaf ears. In a few moments, Sarah and the others were bouncing along in the carriage with a driver as anxious as they were to see the *Arkansas*. When they finally climbed the levee, the ironclad ship called a "ram" lay before them.

"Why look at it! How ugly!" Sarah said, staring in amazement at the awkward metal contraption floating in the river. A square box rose in the center like a great rusty head with cannon poking out like noses.

"Be glad it is on our side. They say this ugly boat caused panic among the Yankees at Vicksburg," Miriam said as she pointed. "See where it is damaged. If it could only sink a few gunboats today, perhaps we could go home."

"Remember that the Yankees also have a ram. The *Essex* will be waiting for our *Arkansas,*" Phillie reminded them.

"Well, God bless and protect her, and the brave men she carries," Sarah whispered.

At the moment those brave and very dirty men were crowded on deck, hastily eating their breakfast. The girls watched until they drifted out of sight, then hurried back to the house. The sound of a furious bombardment was coming from the direction of Baton Rouge. A small upstairs balcony was the best vantage point, and it was soon crowded with ladies. "There it goes! Listen! Look at them!" they shrieked as the cannon balls screamed upward, leaving trails of white smoke.

But as Sarah sat and listened, she wondered which shell might be knocking down her home or killing someone she knew. Tiche and Dophy were supposed to have joined Lilly and the children at Greenwell. Did they get away in time, and remember to turn Jimmy loose?

"See the smoke over the city? It must be on fire," cried Miriam.

"How can you be sure from this distance?" Sarah asked, hating to look from the window.

"We cannot," said Ginnie. "But we can take the carriage for a better view."

Moments later they were rocking down the river road at a pace that made Sarah nauseous. To ease nerves and occupy their hands, the girls had brought a basket of old linen rags to scrape into lint. It would be used to dress wounds, of which there were sure to be many. They soon met other women on the road.

"Go back," one lady warned. "The Yankees are firing on this side of the river as well."

"How does the battle go?" Miriam asked.

"It appears to go well. News is that their General Williams has been killed."

Sarah and Miriam looked at each other sadly.

They rode on until Baton Rouge came in sight. The carriage stopped as a hush fell over the girls. The city still stood, beautiful against the black, lowering sky. Sarah could make out the castle-like State House, the garrison, and the Asylum. But what of the Methodist Church steeple? It was nearest her home—did it still stand?

"There it is!" she cried. "There are no flames near our home. At least not yet."

They watched for a long while before other refugees convinced them of the danger. On the way back explosions from both directions of the river told them that the *Arkansas* and *Essex* must be testing each other's strength. Around the bend in the river came a dark plume of smoke.

"Oh, no! It can't be," cried Ginnie, who sat up front. "The *Arkansas* is on fire!"

The carriage stopped, allowing the girls to climb the outer levee for a better look. Below them, the formidable ironclad belched flames across the water. Smoke rolled across the deck and shells exploded one by one beneath the water, sending up jets of steam. All except Sarah burst into loud sobs. She simply stood, praying silently. With the *Arkansas* went their best hope of reclaiming Baton Rouge.

Over the din voices could be heard coming down the road. The men who came into view were grimy and worn. Some were only half-dressed and carried knapsacks. It was the crew of the *Arkansas*.

"What happened?" the girls cried.

One fellow, looking more energetic than the

rest, ran up to tell them. "We've had engine trouble ever since the fight at Vicksburg. It got down here and just quit. We worked all night to fix it and were ready to meet the *Essex* when the other engine broke. The officers advised the Captain to abandon her, so we set her afire and got off."

"Oh, my, how terrible," the girls chorused as other soldiers stopped. After relating more about their ordeal, the men were ordered to march on. Since many were sick and one was wounded, the girls quickly voted to give them the carriage and walk home. It was gratefully accepted.

As they walked along the levee, the *Essex* came into view, accompanied by two gunboats. Men crowded their decks to watch the *Arkansas* burn. Then they fired one shot apiece and cautiously withdrew.

"I can imagine what glorious accounts they will give of their defeating the *Arkansas*," Sarah said bitterly. But there was nothing more to be done except help the survivors as best they could. Food, drink, and a few firearms were gathered at the plantation for the men until an officer rode up. "Ladies, the Yankee cavalry are after us, and we must fight them in the corn! Take care of yourselves!"

"Yes!" shouted Sarah and the rest. "Hurrah for the *Arkansas* crew! Fight for us. God bless you!"

Two nights later, a great fire lit the sky over Baton

Rouge. Barefoot and in her nightgown, Sarah ran outside to watch. A horrible sinking feeling engulfed her. Was she truly homeless now? General Butler had threatened to burn the town before losing it to the Confederates. That is, when his troops were through stealing and ransacking. With General Williams gone, who would restrain them?

Word had reached the west bank that 84 of General Breckenridge's troops had been killed so far, with 300-400 wounded or captured, and the Union loss was similar. Sarah had also heard that Will Pinkney had been in the attack, and found herself thinking of him often. "I wonder if Will knows I am watching his cannon and praying for him so earnestly? I am sure I would cry if he was hurt," she told Phillie as they listened to the cannon's rumble.

"Why you seem as fond of him as his wife is," Phillie teased.

Sarah was indignant. "Not *quite*. But I knew him first and he has been a good friend. I expect to like him until he proves himself unworthy of my regard—which is not likely."

That was Wednesday. The intermittent sounds of shelling continued through the week until the Nolan household and their guests had almost learned to ignore them. Saturday evening found the women once again reading, sewing, and making lint in the parlor. Charlie had come from "the other side" and taken Miriam to a new refuge at Linwood. Sarah missed her terribly.

Suddenly the terrible whistling of a shell was heard, growing louder by the heartbeat. Sarah sat frozen while the others jumped to their feet, spilling lint and sewing baskets. There was a tremendous "whoosh" overhead as some screamed and covered their heads. Sarah did none of those things. With the loss of home, and family and friends scattered, she was growing indifferent to fear. Except for blowing her to bits, how much more could they do? "A shell," she coolly observed, and went on with her sewing.

High-spirited Ginnie had other ideas. "Come, Sarah. Let's ride down and see who is shooting at us."

Sarah studied the tall girl's wide eyes and flushed cheeks. Ginnie was only fourteen and despite the fact that her father had been taken prisoner seemed to enjoy the excitement the war had brought to her quiet plantation life. Dropping the basket, Sarah followed her out the door, pretending she didn't hear her mother calling through the confusion.

"Sarah Morgan, where are you going? That shell was five feet over this house. This is no time for a frolic. The Yankees will think you are guerrillas. They are shooting at every puff of dust on the road. Sarah, come back!"

Sarah and Ginnie rode on, meeting other people as panicked as her mother. After many warnings and finding no sign of gunboats, they returned home at dusk. Everyone there was almost crazy with worry and had packed to leave. They were in the yard when a flash darted upward.

"See it? Lightning, I expect," Phillie said nervously.

Sarah knew better, but held her tongue. Then came the tearing, hissing sound of a sky rocket—music she had heard before. Instantly she remembered her running bag and flew upstairs after it. The shell burst over the house, rattling down on the gallery. Outside there was bedlam as women screamed and Uncle Will, the carriage driver, tried to calm his plunging horses and shout advice. "Whoa, there! 'Taint safe! Take to the fields! Take to the woods! Run to the sugar house! Take to your heels!"

Chapter 12

❖

Noah's Duck

August 12th

Another resting place! Out of reach of shells for the first time since last April! For how long, I wonder? For wherever we go, we bring shells and Yankees. Would not be surprised at a visit from them out here, now!

Let me take up the thread of that never ending story, and account for my present position. It all seems tame now; but it was very exciting at the time. The other ladies were already in the buggy, leaving Ginnie and me to follow horseback. It was a splendid gallop in the moonlight, over the fields, only it was made uncomfortable by the jerking of my running bag.

A hard ride of four miles in about twenty minutes brought us to the house of the man who so kindly offered his hospitality. It was a little hut, about as large as our parlor, and already crowded to over-flowing, as he was entertaining three families from Baton Rouge. Can't imagine where he put them, either. But it seems to me the poorer the man, and the smaller the house, the greater the hospitality.

I was not sorry when daybreak appeared. When we suggested returning to the Nolan home, all said it was madness; that the Yankees would sack the house and burn it over our heads, we would be insulted, etc.

Sarah glanced at the trunk containing all that she now owned. Despite the warnings, the Morgan women had returned for their things and journeyed further north. She would never forget the stifling heat of that day as they jostled along the rutted road in a wagon bed. Or nervously waiting for a chance to cross the river, now patrolled by the *Essex* and a gunboat.

The ferry they rode slipped across the water just as the ironclad disappeared around a bend, for the ferryman knew the gunboat would not be far behind. Sarah's gaze never left the muddy, swirling water to the south. When they finally reached the east bank, she gasped with relief, wondering if she had held her breath all the way across.

As she lay in another strange bed that night, Sarah wondered how long they would remain homeless, beggars, dependent upon the charity of others. "How are we going to earn a living?" she asked Miriam.

"We could teach," said Miriam. "I could give music lessons and you have certainly read more than any female I know."

Sarah grimaced in the dark. "Teaching is a thankless task. I have never met a governess whom I did not pity."

"Then it is poverty or dependence," Miriam said in her matter-of-fact way.

Sarah thought a moment. "I don't believe poverty would be so disagreeable if it were just you and I. We can make merry in almost any circumstance and will not be the only ones beggared by the war. But it will be hardest on Mother."

Miriam sighed. "I know. Go to sleep now, Sarah."

Sarah flopped over on her stomach. "Well, teaching before dependence, and death before that!"

As August drew to a close, news arrived in snatches from Baton Rouge, none of it good. Finally Charlie decided to return and, despite his protests, Sarah went along. It was a long, incredibly bumpy ride down the muddy road in the small, low-necked buggy. A pungent odor drifted on the morning breeze as Sarah wrinkled her nose. "What is that horrid smell?" she tried to ask without breathing.

Charlie pointed ahead. "This is the same route our soldiers took when they attacked the city. The first Yankee camp is just ahead—or what is left of it. Your friend Will Pinkney and Colonel Bird set fire to it the day of the battle."

Sarah nodded, feeling quite proud of Will's exploits as they rounded the next curve. Then, she gasped. Charred wood, burnt clothes, tents, and all imaginable articles were strewn in every direction.

Fresh earth formed two mounds in ditches on either side of the road, as if marking the entrance to a graveyard. Beyond were more mounds, some with a hand or foot exposed as rain had settled the dirt. The smell was overwhelming. Sarah buried her face in her handkerchief for just ahead lay the skeleton of a man whose horse had fallen on him.

The road wound through two more wrecked Yankee camps before reaching Baton Rouge. Sarah hardly recognized her town. Felled trees blocked the streets, and many fine buildings were reduced to crumbling walls. Charlie clucked to the horse as they neared Church Street, only to find it blocked. Going around another way, Sarah saw that the nice brick cottage facing their back lot was gone.

"Charlie, look!" she cried. "God has spared our home!" Sarah jumped from the buggy and ran through the yard. The doors to the storage and servants' quarters hung open, but she didn't pause until reaching her own front door. Taking a deep breath, she stepped inside and froze in amazement.

Before her lay a scene of total ruin. The sideboards had been split open with axes and china smashed on the floor. Muddy footprints adorned the sofa; portraits had been pulled down and shredded from their frames. Bookshelves were empty and papers were scattered everywhere.

Charlie joined her and could only say, "Well?"

Though sick at heart, Sarah felt a laugh well up inside and burst forth in spite of herself. "It is so absurd, Charlie. Since we were not here, they made war on our *things*." She wandered to the corner where her favorite rocker and papier-mâché sewing box had sat. Both were gone. "To think that Abraham Lincoln's soldiers would steal in such a wholesale manner. What do they want with my knitting needles?"

Upstairs in her room, Sarah found that her small paradise there was gone as well. The only dresses that remained looked at though someone had pierced them with a bayonet. The desk had been broken into, and the letters she had not carried away were scattered about. Her toilet stand and armoire were smashed. The tall mirror stood squinting at her from a thousand broken angles. She paused there, thinking how many times she and Miriam had smoothed their hair before it.

"Well, I am beggared," she told the reflection. "Strange to say, I don't feel it. Perhaps it is the satisfaction of knowing my fate that makes me so cheerful."

Later, as she packed the few unbroken items, an old fellow who looked after her aunt's property stopped by. "It was two Yankee officers did all the mischief," he told Sarah and Charlie. "Ripped the place apart thinkin' you ladies was hidin' somewhere. I told 'em, 'Ain't you 'shamed to destroy all this here, that belongs to a poor widow lady who's got two daughters to support?'"

Charles Barker shook his gray head sadly. "They said from the looks of this furniture, them Secesh women must not be too poor. I ran out to the street and found a Captain who hauled 'em off, but it was too late."

"Thank you for trying, Charles. I know Mother will be grateful," Sarah told him. It pleased her to know that while some five thousand former slaves in the area had been freed and told to follow the Yankee officers, the Morgan servants had remained. She wasn't sure if it was loyalty, affection, or simply no better place to go, but she considered them all beyond praise.

Charles went on. "Yes'm. Oh, and I got your little bird. When the shells was flyin', Tiche ran off and forgot him. He's been sharin' my cornbread ever since."

"You have Jimmy? Oh, bless you, Charles!" Sarah clapped her hands, and for the first time that day, a tear slipped out—a tear of joy.

August 29. Clinton, La.

Noah's duck has found another resting place! Yesterday I was interrupted while writing to pack up for another move, it being impossible to find a boarding house in the neighborhood. We heard of some about here, and Charlie had engaged a house for his family, where the servants were already settled, so I hurried off to my task. I had a severe task of trunk packing, one of my greatest delights. I hate to see anyone pack loosely or in a slovenly manner. Perhaps this is the reason I never let anyone do it, if I am able to stand.

We started off again, General Carter driving me in his buggy. I love General Carter. A better or kinder man than he does not live. After so many kind invitations, he told me he was sorry we would not remain with him at Linwood, and spoke so kindly, that I felt as though I had a Yankee ball in my throat. I was disposed to be melancholy anyway; I could not say many words without choking. I was going from the kindest of friends to a country where I had none at all.

As we reached the track, the train cars came shrieking along. There was a pause, a scuffle during which the General placed me and my bird in a seat, while Lilly, Charles, Miriam, mother, five children and two servants, with all the baggage, were thrown aboard some way. With a shriek and a jerk we were off again.

I enjoyed that ride. It had but one fault; and that was, that it came to an end. I would have wished for it to spin along until the war was over, or we in a settled home. But it ended at last, to Jimmy's great relief; for he was too frightened to move even, and only ventured a timid chirp if the car stopped, as though to ask, "Is it over?" Nothing occurred of any interest except once a little boy sent us slightly off the track by meddling with the brakes. Landed at sunset, it is hard to fancy a more forlorn crew while waiting at the depot to get the baggage. We burst out laughing as we looked at each lengthened face. Such a procession through the straggling village as we trudged through the hilly streets—they have no pavement here—looking like emigrants from the Ould Country, as we have watched them in New Orleans.

Finally reaching the small, unfurnished house

Charlie had secured, they found Tiche laid up from an accident. While they were crossing one of the smaller rivers, part of the bridge had given way with the Morgan servants and their loaded wagon. All four mules, three grown people, and four children had fallen twenty feet into the deep water below. Thankfully, not a life was lost. The mattress on which everyone sat floated them into shallow water. Tiche had been the only casualty, with a severely sprained leg. Even the baggage, though soaked, was saved.

Dinner was eaten sitting on the floor. With no glasses and little silverware, Sarah discovered that cornbread could be eaten with her fingers and water drunk from a cup. How she missed bread made with flour and real coffee. It was also obvious that some of the family would have to find other lodging, for the low-ceilinged house with its four small rooms was suffocating.

Stretching her weary limbs, Sarah decided that "Noah's duck" should be the first to volunteer.

Chapter 13

❖

Homeless

September 1st. Monday.

I wake up this morning and, to my great surprise, find that we have already entered the first month of fall. Where has the summer gone to? The days have gone by like a dream. I am content to let the time fly, though, as every day brings us nearer Peace—or something else.

"How shockingly I write," Sarah muttered, noticing that her usually neat script had gone awry. Would she ever have a desk or table to write on again? She squirmed, shifting her position on the mattress, which served for sleeping, eating, and sitting. The homemade candle flickered and threw shadows that danced on the windowless wall. "I wish Mother would carry out her threat and brave the occasional shellings at Baton Rouge," she told Miriam, who was trying to sleep. "I would dare anything to be home again, as bare as it is."

"I miss my piano," Miriam mumbled.

"I miss my workbasket and dumb bells—and the shoes I paid five dollars for and wore a single time. Now I am almost barefooted, and cannot find a pair in the whole country."

"Would it not be curious, if one of these days while traveling in the North . . ."

"If we ever travel again," Sarah interrupted.

"If we ever travel again, that we should find some well-loved object in a strange house as a 'Trophy of the Battle of Baton Rouge'?"

Sarah pondered. "It would have to be in some very low house, for surely respectable people would have nothing to do with such work. I wonder if they would have the conscience to return it?"

As the days hovered between summer and fall, Sarah became well acquainted with the pastoral sights around tiny Clinton. Finding items necessary for existence was an even greater challenge than it had been in Baton Rouge.

"Ouf! What a country!" she said, leaving the small general store with Lilly and Dellie. "I am ready to ask some clerk, out of curiosity, what they *do* sell in Clinton. That man actually laughed when I asked for candles and bird seed."

Lilly sighed. "It is the same for most of my list—glasses, flour, soap, starch, coffee."

"I think my first act on returning home will be to have a cup of coffee and a piece of wheat bread. Miriam vows to devour an unheard of number of biscuits," said Sarah.

"I am tired of vegetables," Dellie complained. "I

don't like snap beans and tomatoes."

"Be thankful we can get them," Lilly reminded her. "You will cultivate the taste."

Sarah winked at her niece. "We would rather cultivate our tastes for sponge cake and ice cream."

Dellie vigorously agreed.

"I don't remember the last time we had ice cream," said Lilly.

"A year ago last July," said Sarah. "And we had ice nine months out of the year. The only ice I have seen this year was in a hailstorm."

"There is no point in dwelling on what we cannot have," Lilly said in a voice that sounded older with each passing day. "Perhaps this shop will at least have piece goods. Morgan is bursting out of his shirts."

They entered the next store, where shelves were not as bare as the previous one. Looking at the prices, Sarah knew why. Her brother in New Orleans had managed to send Mother some money, although they had no idea how long it would last. She studied the collection of buttons and missed her workbasket more than ever with its bits of lace and embroidery.

The door jingled, admitting two officers who also studied the piece goods. One held up a bolt of dark blue merino wool. "Pardon me, ma'am, but could you give me some advice?"

Lilly nodded.

"How much of this should I purchase for a new

shirt? Mine have seen better days," he said, ruefully picking at a threadbare spot.

Sarah tried not to smile as Lilly carefully explained the principles of measuring and cutting fabric. The second officer listened attentively. "Who will be sewing this for you?" Lilly asked.

The first officer blushed as he shrugged. "I suppose we will. We have acquired many domestic talents since this war began."

Lilly smiled. "I am sure you have. But since defending Port Hudson is the more pressing duty, perhaps you will allow us to sew these for you."

"Oh, no, that would be too much of an imposition," the officer protested.

"Nonsense. It is the least we can do for our soldiers," said Lilly.

Sarah nodded in agreement, and after more protests, the men consented and purchased what was needed for two handsome new dress shirts. She was glad to have a project and purpose for the next few days.

Sunday Sept 14th 1862.

I have been so busy making Lieut. Bourge's shirt that I have not had time to write, besides having very little to write about. I would not let any one touch Lieut. Bourge's shirt, except myself; and last evening when I held it up completed, the loud praises it received satisfied me it would answer. Miriam and Mrs. Ripley declared it the prettiest ever made. I should first hear the opinion of the owner, though. If he does not agree with all the others, I shall say he has no taste.

Linwood. Sept 17th. Wednesday.

Still floating about! This morning after breakfast General Carter made his appearance, and in answer to his question as to whether we were ready to leave with him, Miriam replied, "Yes indeed" heartily. Though glad to leave Clinton, I was sorry to part with Mother. I could not leave my bird in that house. He has never sung since I recovered him.

We had a very pleasant ride as we had very agreeable company. The train only stopped thirteen times in the twenty miles. Five times to clear the brushwood from the telegraph lines, once running back a mile to pick up a passenger, and so on, to the great indignation of many passengers aboard. The General gravely assured them that it was an old habit of this very accommodating train, which in summer time, stopped when ever the passengers wished to pick blackberries on the road.

Many soldiers were aboard on their way to Port Hudson to rejoin their companies. One gallant one offered me a drink of water from his canteen, which I accepted out of mere curiosity to see what water from such a source tasted of. To my great surprise, I found it tasted just like any other.

Though worried about Mother and Lilly, Sarah and Miriam soon settled into Linwood's routine. They had always enjoyed time spent with the Carters, whose daughter Lydia had married their brother Gibbes. The General's sister, Mrs. Badger, was also staying there with her children.Noisy Anna, the sixteen-year-old, shared a large upstairs room with the Morgan girls.

The dignified white house, modest by plantation standards, was never quiet or lonely. It was surrounded by five thousand rolling acres of forest, pasture, and sugar cane fields. Situated about twenty miles north of Baton Rouge, Linwood was on the river, and crops were shipped out by a railroad spur.

It was also five miles from Port Hudson, one of the last two Confederate strongholds on the river. Troops passed daily, gathering there to meet the Yankee offensive that was sure to come. Some straggled by on foot, while others hopped off at the train stop to ask for a meal. When a large group from Mississippi stopped for water one afternoon, Sarah helped the servants fill the many canteens. She was surprised to find most of the men carrying wire-and-canvas Yankee canteens with neat stoppers instead of the flat tin Confederate variety.

"Thank you, miss. You're mighty kind," came the profusion of thanks. On the gallery, Mother tended a soldier from the *Arkansas* who suffered with a fever while the other girls held plates for those too weak to eat. Sarah smiled as she emptied her bucket, thinking how blessed was the Confederate soldier when sympathetic women were near!

The next day was quieter, with a constant drizzle from clouds as watery as New Orleans milk. The house grew smaller as the young people grew restless. Finally Mrs. Carter suggested making molasses candy, which sent them out back to the kitchen. After a great deal of pot-watching and fin-ger-licking, the candy was ready to pull. Sarah pulled until her arms ached. The results were worth it, however, and after eating her share and washing sticky hands, she noticed that the rain had stopped.

"At last! We can get a little fresh air before the sun is gone."

"We can do more than that," said Anna. "Let's take the pony cart out."

As the three set out for the cart, their mothers protested, "Girls! Soap is a dollar and a half a bar and starch a dollar a pound. Take up those skirts!"

Trying to avoid the worst of the mud, they lifted their stiff, full skirts. Fortunately, there were no men around to see how high. Anna turned, trying to see behind her. "Is mine touching the mud?" she asked.

"Not unless you sit down," Sarah teased her.

The pony, appropriately named Tom Thumb, was led down the long brick drive to the slaves' cabins where the cart was used for hauling wood. A boy not much bigger than the pony was drafted into driving, and they were off. At a neighbor's house a group of children piled on, raising the number in the cart to eleven. The pony strained as the cart groaned and creaked through the mud, but continued until they were some distance from the house.

"Turn him around," Miriam called. "We should head back."

The boy pulled and tugged and shook the long

reins, with no response. Tom Thumb plowed on in ever-widening circles until they stopped, completely bogged down. The driver went to tug on the pony's bridle as the children gleefully hopped out.

"It is nearly dark. Won't we get it at home?" groaned Anna.

"What will the General say?" Miriam laughed.

Sarah sighed. "And Mrs. Carter." She helped tug at the pony while the remaining bit of daylight slipped away.

At last a buggy appeared carrying two men. With a quick "heave-ho," the men freed the cart. Finding himself free to move, the pony trotted away. "Wait," cried the girls as they fished the seven children from the mud and pursued the flying hooves.

It was late before the children were deposited and the girls returned home in their muddy, bedraggled glory. "Maybe we can just slip up to bed," Miriam suggested.

"Without supper?" responded Anna. "I am famished. But perhaps we should change shoes before the General sees us."

"Well, the worst he can do is prohibit future rides," said Sarah.

Taking their shoes off on the back steps, they slipped in the door. Then Miriam squared her shoulders and sauntered into the parlor with her most carefree laugh. "Good evening, General, Mrs. Carter. You won't believe what happened to us!"

As the story was told in her most hilarious

manner, Sarah had to admire her sister's boldness. Miriam was rarely bothered by things that Sarah had struggled to overcome as she had grown up—shyness, fear of strangers, poor self-esteem. When Miriam had devoted herself to the piano, Sarah had ceased to practice. When Miriam learned to play the guitar, Sarah had refused to compete, although their music teacher insisted she was the better musician. When Miriam's suitors were turned away, they would turn to Sarah as friend and confidant. It was how she had become close to Will Pinkney years before.

But tonight Miriam's magic charmed the older folks into forgetting the girls' late return and dirty clothes. Perhaps their foolishness was a welcome relief to the grim realities that surrounded them all.

Chapter 14

❖

Linwood

The pleasant autumn days flew by. They were the happiest Sarah had known in a long while. It was cane-cutting time on the plantation, and except for the passing of soldiers, the war seemed far away. The girls entertained themselves with long horseback rides along the river, or took their favorite books and donned rubber boots for a walk in the quiet woods. Wherever they went, someone would bring a purple stalk of sugar cane for cutting and chewing. Even the most refined ladies enjoyed chewing the sweet pulp until the juice was gone, then disposing of it in some civilized manner.

Other foods were more plentiful than they had been in Clinton, and Miriam finally had enough biscuits to eat. In the evening, the girls might pop corn or make candy in their bedroom's open fireplace. After the long weeks cooped up during the trouble in town, Sarah found herself thriving on the fresh country air, exercise, and good food. Her usually pale cheeks were turning brown, and her clothes were getting tight.

"Look at this," she told Miriam one afternoon. "Mrs. Carter will no longer be able to pinch my waist with her two hands. Perhaps I will yet be obliged to wear corsets to make me look smaller instead of larger, as I have been."

"Well, hurry and tie it, whatever your motive," Miriam told her. "We must leave soon or miss the dress parade."

"Almost ready," Sarah said, slipping on her pink-and-white muslin dress and pinning on the only hat the Yankees had left her. It was a black straw walking hat adorned with black ribbon and sheaves of wheat. They did not match perfectly, but people seemed less critical of fashion these days. Everyone wore "Confederate dresses," meaning last year's style. It was the same with other things—"Confederate silver" meant a tin cup or spoon, a "Confederate bridle" was a rope halter, and "Confederate flour" meant corn meal.

Outside, a group had gathered to admire a mule-drawn wagon with four seats and a leather-covered top. The General addressed them with a flourish. "Young ladies, if you will ride in a Confederate carriage, you may now go to dress parade."

The girls laughed and climbed in with Mrs. Badger as their chaperone. The five-mile ride was a pleasant one, but as they approached the camps surrounding the bustling town of Port Hudson, Sarah grew apprehensive. Men were everywhere, and it seemed all eyes were riveted on the carriage.

"I should have stayed home," Sarah whispered to Miriam.

"Nonsense," Miriam replied. "Look, they are about to start."

As orders were barked and men of the 4th Louisiana fell in line, Sarah's heart went out to the bedraggled lot. Many of these soldiers who had fought at Shiloh and Baton Rouge were barefoot and dressed in rags. Even the officers were clad only in cotton pants, flannel shirts, and jackets far too short. Hats were of every style and shape, making it a colorful parade indeed.

They passed other groups before reaching a beautiful open common. The 30th Louisiana was drilling there, but Sarah hardly noticed. She was staring at the tents—hundreds of them. She wondered if George and Gibbes lived in similar circumstances, and if it were as dreadful as it looked. Yet there were barefoot soldiers tossing caps and chasing two old gray geese as if they were boys just out of school.

The commander, Col. Gustave Breaux, greeted the girls warmly. Sarah remembered his stopping at Linwood for dinner and then showing up in church on Sunday. The eloquent colonel had been a New Orleans attorney before the war and had performed admirably in the Battle of Baton Rouge. They talked until the sun sank behind the trees and campfires, looking like giant fireflies across the hills, were lit.

The following week Colonel Breaux and another officer took the girls on a tour of the extensive fortifications the soldiers were building around Port Hudson. They rode this time, Sarah's ride made more thrilling by the strong, handsome horse she was mounted on. As they watched the Mississippi from the edge of a high bluff, she fancied how easily he could plunge into the muddy water below, and she would be powerless to stop him.

The Colonel proved to be a pleasant companion, one who spoke as though he believed her intelligent enough to appreciate whatever subject he was discussing. After the ride, the officers were invited to supper at Linwood where conversation continued. Sarah discovered that Colonel Breaux knew a great deal about many subjects, from philosophy to health to gardening. He expressed himself so beautifully that Sarah was amazed to learn he had not learned to speak English until age fourteen. She listened with her eyes, ears, and all her soul. No one had talked with her this way since Father and Harry died.

It was late when the guests left, and as they dressed for bed, the girls were still discussing the Colonel. "He is indeed charming," said Miriam. "Why must all the nice men be married?"

Usually Sarah would have laughed at that comment, but another thought troubled her as she climbed into bed—that of her own ignorance. It made her feel painfully inferior in the presence of one someone like Colonel Breaux.

Why was I denied the education that would enable me to be the equal of such men? she cried to herself. *He says the woman's mind is the same as the man's, originally; it is only education that creates the difference. Why was I denied that education?*

Who is to blame? Have I exerted fully the natural desire To Know that is implanted in all hearts? Have I done myself injustice or has injustice been done to me? Whose is the fault? Have I labored to improve the few opportunities thrown in my path to the best of my ability?

Answer for yourself, Sarah. With the exception of ten short months at school where you learned nothing except Arithmetic, you have been your own teacher, your own scholar, all your life, after which you were taught by Mother the elements of reading and writing. Give an account of your charge. What do you know? Nothing! Except that I am a fool!

Sarah buried her face in the sheet, not wanting even the darkness to see her humiliation.

———— ❖ ————

"Sarah, wake up!" It was Miriam.

"What?" Sarah rolled over and rubbed her puffy eyes.

"A dispatch just arrived from Gibbes in Mobile. He is on his way home!"

"How wonderful!" Sarah gave Miriam a joyful hug, then paused. "But what can bring him here? Oh, Miriam, he must be wounded."

Miriam nodded. "That is what Lydia fears. She has gone to meet his train in Clinton."

The next three days dragged by. The girls stayed near the house, knowing their brother might arrive at any hour. Sarah paced up and down the dirt road on which the carriage would come. Every wagon rattling through the field made them stop and listen; every cane stalk waving in the moon-light brought them to their feet. At last, after supper, far off in the clear light they saw the carriage. Unable to sit still, Sarah went to stand under the tree where it would stop. Anna followed, much to her annoyance. It had been seventeen months since she had seen Gibbes, and she was determined to be the first to greet him.

"Don't drag him out of the carriage now," cautioned Eugene Carter, Lydia's brother. "You don't know how badly he may be wounded."

Sarah said nothing, straining to see down the road.

"Of course, it could be someone else," Eugene teased.

"Then I suppose they shall get a kiss," Sarah said, nervously shufflling from one foot to the other.

Finally the carriage came around the circle. Before she saw his face, Sarah heard her brother's voice. "Gibbes! Gibbes!" she cried as it rolled to a stop.

"My darling!" he said, and in a moment his strong right arm was wrapped around her. The left hung in a sling. Sarah could say no more for her heart was in her throat. She could not remember being so happy.

The rest of the family clustered around, hugging, kissing, grabbing the well hand while avoiding the other one. "How bad is it?" they would ask. "Just a scratch," Gibbes would answer. When he was settled in a chair on the balcony, Sarah pulled off his hat and coat and knelt in front, her arm across his lap. Like her, Miriam and Lydia could not get close enough.

As the news spread across Linwood, many of the workers came to greet him as well. "How is you, Mass' Gibbes?" was heard in all imaginable keys and accents, while Gibbes greeted each and inquired into their own state of health.

"I suppose even wounded soldiers can eat," Mrs. Carter finally announced, so supper was again prepared. Sarah was only too eager to butter the cornbread, spread the preserves, and carve the mutton. Gibbes thanked her for the help, but she wondered if it could be so pleasant to a strong man accustomed to taking care of himself.

When all had settled down to talk, Sarah noticed that the usually energetic Gibbes talked in a slow, deliberate manner that spoke of suffering. "Where were you wounded?" everyone wanted to know.

"At Sharpsburg on the 17th of September at nine in the morning," he told them. Despite the many questions, that was all he told them of his own experiences. "They say George was there, and came out safe, though I never saw him. Our army, having accomplished its objective, recrossed the Potomac after what was a decidedly drawn battle. Both sides suffered severely. Hardly an officer on either side escaped unhurt. I expect the list will contain the names of many friends."

As the others questioned him, Sarah smuggled in an atlas and turned to the map of Virginia. "Show me where you were," she begged.

Gibbes traced Stonewall Jackson's campaign as

well as the small map would allow. Then he told of the heroic deeds of his fellow soldiers—but of his own, not a word. Sarah knew that her brother was among the bravest of the brave, but respected him all the more for his silence.

Mrs. Badger interrupted them by insisting it was time to dress Gibbes' wound and let him get some rest. It was late before Sarah pulled out her diary.

Oct 4th. Saturday.

I have just come from seeing Gibbes' wound dressed. If that is a scratch, Heaven defend me from wounds! A minie ball struck his left shoulder strap, which caused it to glance, thereby saving the bone. Just above, in the the fleshy part it tore the flesh off in a strip three inches and a half, by two. Such a great raw, green, pulpy wound, bound around by a heavy red ridge of flesh! Mrs. Badger, who dressed it, turned sick; Miriam turned away groaning; servants exclaimed with horror; it was the first experience of any, except Mrs. Badger, in wounds.

I wanted to try my nerves, so I held the towel around his body and kept the flies off while it was being washed. It is so offensive that the water trickling on my dress has obliged me to change it. He talked all the time, ridiculing the groans of sympathy over a "scratch." O how I loved him for his fortitude!

Chapter 15

❖

Runaway

Sunday 26th Oct.

Every one having gone to church except Lydia and me, I have at last a leisure moment. Closing the door, with my feet in the fire (for it turned extremely cold yesterday, and there is ice this morning), I shall take advantage of the unnatural quiet to write—if I can find a writing table. This writing on one's knee does not improve the handwriting, as this whole book can testify. I suppose by the time I get back to my desk I will not be able to write at all.

This place is completely over run by soldiers passing and repassing. Friday night five stayed here, last night two more, and another has just gone. One, a bashful Tennesseean, had never tasted sugar cane. We were sitting around a blazing fire, enjoying it hugely, when in answer to our repeated invitations to help himself, he confessed he had never eaten it. Once instructed, though, he got on remarkably well and ate in a civilized manner, considering it was his first attempt.

Every thing points to a speedy attack on Port Hudson. Rumors reach us from New Orleans of extensive preparations by land and water, and of the determination to burn Clinton in revenge for the looms that were carried from Baton Rouge there. They can soon be put in working order to supply our soldiers, negroes, and ourselves with necessary clothing.

Company, company! is so constantly the cry.

The stream of visitors continued. Some came to see General Carter or Gibbes, or perhaps enjoy a home-cooked meal. However, Mrs. Badger observed that the three unmarried young ladies were Linwood's greatest attraction. Whenever the officers were granted a pass, they seemed undaunted by the five-mile ride. While Sarah found a few of the men to be amiable company, Anna and Miriam thoroughly enjoyed the attention. Will Carter, the General's nephew, who had always liked Miriam, began calling more often, to Sarah's annoyance. Will was loud, boisterous, and known to drink too much—certainly not the perfect man for her Miriam.

There was activity in the fields as well. After cane was cut, it was hauled in wagons to the sugar house for grinding. Sometimes the girls rode perched on top of the cane, singing "Dye My Petticoats" to the General's great amusement. The long purple stalks were then ground to extract the juice, which was boiled in huge kettles.

One evening when Linwood was filled with company (Sarah counted eighteen in the parlor alone), the General told her to bring the young people to the sugar house. It was a cold walk in the moonlight down the gently sloping hill. The three-story structure was lit inside with "Confederate gas," or pine torches, which shed a friendly light over a row of kettles. Dusky Negroes leaned over them in the steam, lightly turning their paddles in the foamy syrup. When the guests asked to try their hands at stirring, the workers became instructors. As Sarah watched them laugh at the beginners and join in the fun, it occurred to her that if Abe Lincoln could spend grinding season on a plantation he would recall his Proclamation. Never in her home, nor at Linwood, had she seen the cruelty abolitionists railed about, and the dark faces that joined her silly songs seemed far from miserable. Life would certainly not be the same without them.

When all hands were appropriately sticky, someone suggested a game of "Puss Wants a Corner." As the young people jostled and raced to occupy their corners, all dignity was discarded. They laughed and ran as fast as any children, and it was obvious that the General enjoyed the fun as much anyone. Forfeits followed, with losers given absurd penalties. One fellow had to ride a barrel, while a new acquaintance, Frank Enders, had to kiss Sarah's hand. He made no objection.

It was past midnight when Mrs. Badger horrified all by ordering them to retire. Sarah was surprised to find the *nuage* she had discarded tied around Mr. Enders' neck. He refused to give it back. "It will be at Port Hudson awaiting your next visit," he teased.

The other girls giggled and even Sarah had to laugh. "Very well," she said. "How shall we find you?"

The next week passed with more wagon rides, company, and sugar making. A Morgan cousin, Henry Gibbes, had joined the soldiers at Port Hudson, and a trip was planned to see him and Frank Enders. Since no men were available to drive them, Miriam and Anna took one carriage while Sarah rode with Mrs. Badger. Remembering her embarrassment at being stared at by hundreds of eyes, Sarah wore a thick veil and promised herself that this would be her last trip to the camp.

However, Cousin Henry Gibbes was delighted to see them, and the visit was more pleasant than she had expected. He then hopped in Miriam's buggy to drive them to Frank's medical unit. Sarah and Mrs. Badger were following them past an Alabama regiment on parade when a gun discharged. The horse bolted. Despite Mrs. Badger's pull on the reins, it was soon in a dead run. Sarah did not cry out, for she felt confident the woman could hold him as long as the bridle lasted. Since there was nothing to hold onto in the low-neck buggy and jumping out was even more dangerous, she sat quietly, hands in her lap. Perhaps the horse would tire soon.

Then, up near the horse's head, the left rein snapped. Sarah took a deep breath, for death seemed inevitable. Yet she remained quiet, determined to face it calmly. Then the horse swerved abruptly and she was propelled forward. Mrs. Badger's white cape fluttered above her and something struck her lower spine hard.

Sarah cried out, thinking the pain would kill her before she reached the ground. But reach it she did, landing hard on her left side to face the spinning wheels of the capsized buggy. There was a rush of horses and men galloping up. Sarah would have given worlds to spring to her feet, or at least see if they were exposed, but found she could not move. She had no more power over her limbs than if they were made of iron; only the intense pain told her that she was still alive.

She wondered where Miriam was, wanting her to come. Iinstead, a soldier leaped from his horse and leaned over to help. His excited horse reared and Sarah had a vision of iron-shod hooves. Death was certain this time, but she could not move. The soldier jumped up and struck the horse, who turned aside as he came to earth.

As Sarah struggled to move, to breathe, it seemed that thirty pairs of soldier arms were stretched out to help. "No, Gibbes! Gibbes!" she protested. Cousin Henry Gibbes was trembling even more than Sarah as he held her up.

"Send for the doctor!" someone cried. "A surgeon, quick!"

"Tell them no," Sarah whispered. There was a clatter of hooves and cloud of dust as a soldier amazed everyone by bringing a glass of water at a full gallop. She drank it, growing more conscious of the unwanted attention than she was of the pain. Miriam and Anna were beside her now, voices quavering between fear and laughter.

"Sarah, are you all right? Can you move at all?" Miriam asked.

Sarah was trying to answer when the young Alabamian who had first reached her exclaimed, "It was the most beautiful somerset I ever saw! Indeed, it could not be more gracefully done. Your feet did not show!"

Sarah sighed with relief for that was exactly what she wanted to know. Suddenly the absurdity of the scene hit her full force and she began to laugh. As if they had been awaiting permission, Miriam and Anna giggled and many of the soldiers smiled. All around her the comments flew, "The young lady is seriously injured, only she won't acknowledge it. She is the coolest, most dignified girl you ever saw. The prettiest auburn hair you ever looked at. See how it sweeps the ground."

Even Sarah was laughing as a path was cleared for the camp's doctor. Miriam got herself under control first. "Hush, before you go into hysterics," she told Sarah.

Hearing her, one of the men shouted, "Doctor, Doctor Madding! Can't you do something? Is she going to have hysterics?"

Sarah sobered as the young doctor knelt beside her. "Where does it hurt, miss?" he asked.

"Her lower back," Miriam informed him. "She cannot move."

The doctor's hand started out, then froze in midair as he realized the part of her anatomy he was about to examine. Stiffening like a lion at bay, Sarah waved her hand in protest. Judging from the pain, she suspected that the lower tip of her spine was broken. But to be examined before this crowd—never!

The redfaced Dr. Madding withdrew his hand. "The ambulance is coming, miss. Would you prefer to go home?"

Sarah relaxed and nodded. Soon the conveyance arrived and with her cousin's assistance, she managed to get inside. Mrs. Badger, whose only casualty was a torn dress, also climbed in. It was then that Frank Enders arrived. "I was tending a patient when a man came for the ambulance," he said breathlessly. "He said a young lady with the prettiest auburn hair had had a dreadful accident. When he mentioned auburn hair, I knew it had to be you."

After making Sarah as comfortable as possible, they began the painful, bumpy ride home. Outside, there were many goodbyes. "Take care, miss," called the boy from Alabama. "I was proud to be the first to assist you."

The stately white columns of Linwood were a welcome sight. Sarah was met with sympathetic faces and somehow helped up the steep stairway. A dozen hands undressed her to lie face down on the bed. There she stayed, unable to turn, for the slightest motion was torture. The story was retold many times in the days that followed, and missing her diary, Sarah devised a way to write propped on one arm.

Saturday Nov. 15th

I think I grow no better rapidly. Fortunately on Wednesday night they succeeded in turning me over. My poor elbows, having lost all their skin, were completely used up. Now, if I go slowly and carefully, I can turn myself at the cost of some little suffering. I am well enough off, for there is my dinner that I can eat, if I only had the appetite, and there are books to read when I get tired of doing nothing.

There is poor Anna who was taken with a slight fever the day after I was laid up, who has been there ever since unable to eat or read, and who groans loudly enough for forty. I think hers is the least enviable position.

Yesterday Colonel Steedman of the 1st Alabama called with the rather unpleasant advice to be cupped and scarified. His profession was that of a physician before he became Colonel. More messages of condolence and sympathy upstairs, which produced no visible effect on my spine, though very comforting to the spirit.

Ah me! how much more cheerfully I would have borne the breaking of an arm. I may do myself the justice to say that I make no complaints, and am always ready for a laugh. But I would gladly exchange the back for an arm. Merciful Father, let me walk once more! Anything save a helpless cripple.

In the days that followed, Sarah was subject to

the latest forms of medical torture as the swelling on her spine was repeatedly cut and suctioned. A Dr. Dortch brought a new instrument for the procedure in which two dozen shiny teeth were buried in the flesh. As large suction cups drew out blood, Sarah made her audience laugh. "Where did you find such powerful cups? They have loosened the roots of my teeth, and I daresay have pulled my hair in at least a foot!"

Even in the busy household, some evenings were lonely as company was entertained downstairs. Though many of the officers came as before, Sarah refused to see gentlemen in her bedroom. Instead there were notes, messages, and flowers from Frank and others. A determined Will Carter sent candy, and on his seventh visit did not ask permission, but simply walked upstairs. Sarah prefered the candy to his company.

Hearing of her misfortune, Lilly came on the cars from Clinton for a visit. Her visit was far too short for Sarah, who was especially touched by the pralines Dellie had sent. With Lilly came news of other family members. Their sister Lavinia in California had given birth to a daughter three months before, George was well, and Jimmy was on a ship in the Bermudas. As much as she missed them all, Sarah was grateful that they could not see her just now, crippled and helpless.

Tuesday 25th. Night.

The General sends word he has tried in vain to

discover the man who fired that unlucky gun, to punish him for it. I hope he will never find him. What good would it do? No punishment they could inflict on him would heal my poor spine. The Doctor confesses that he fears it is beyond his skill, and that it is more serious than I allow others to suppose.

What then? Am I to be a cripple for life? O my God! I who love earth and air so much, who am never so happy as when wandering alone with Thee and Nature, is this to be my end? Am I to depend on others for each little office I was once so proud of being able to perform for myself? My heart swells when Gibbes looks at me so sadly. Shall Miriam, so fond of pleasure, be chained down by my sick bed, with my miserable pale face to haunt her where ever she goes and mar all enjoyment? Dear Lord! For their sake let death come first. I could stand it better than this torturing helplessness that gives such pain to others.

Chapter 16

❖

The Bride

As December began, Sarah was delighted to find that she could once again stand alone. The simple act renewed her hope and made getting dressed a much easier chore. Loneliness and Mrs. Badger convinced her to try going downstairs, so she was carried down the narrow stairwell to sit in a large wheeled chair in the parlor.

Everyone seemed determined to make Sarah's first trip down a pleasant one as Frank Enders pushed the chair wherever she wished. She preferred being near the piano. There Miriam played and the three of them sang, entertaining the rest of the household.

They were interrupted by a knock at the front door, followed by Lydia bringing in a large bundle. "Miriam, this is for you."

Miriam read the attached note and, going slightly pale, unwrapped the bundle.

"What is it?" asked Sarah.

"A bridal suit," Miriam said slowly. "Only worn once."

"A what? Who sent it?"

"A lady from Clinton who was at the card game."

"What card game?"

Lydia burst out laughing as Miriam smiled. "Remember the Tableaux Vivants we went to in Jackson?" she asked.

Sarah remembered, for she had spent a lonely two days while everyone attended a "Living Pictures" event to benefit the Soldiers' Hospital.

"There was a party afterward. Will Carter and I were playing cards and . . . well, I staked myself in the game."

"You did *what?*"

Miriam giggled. "I wagered Will that if he won, I would marry him."

Sarah's mouth fell open. "Miriam! And you lost?"

"Yes, but it was all in jest," Miriam protested. "He knew that."

"So this bridal suit is part of the joke?"

Frank spoke up. "I think it may be a sincere gesture. Will has announced the engagement all over Clinton. The word is that he plans to claim his bride immediately."

Sarah shook her head in disbelief. "Why have I not been told? Miriam, how could you be so foolish? Will is insane about you. There is no telling what he might do."

They were interrupted by a stir in the foyer. It was Mr. Garie, the local minister, trying to scrape mud from his boots. Lydia greeted him and continued to laugh so hard that she could hardly introduce him.

"Good evening, ladies. I understand there is to be a wedding," the man said through chattering teeth. "Ten miles through mud and water, but glad to do it on such a happy occasion. Far too few of them these days."

Sarah held her breath, waiting to see what Miriam would do. Lydia tried to control herself as Gibbes and General Carter came to see what the noise was about. After greeting the minister, they returned to their cigars, disgusted with the whole affair. Will was the General's nephew and Gibbes' in-law. Neither wished to take sides against him.

"You are freezing, Mr. Garie. Please come warm yourself," said Miriam, walking to the fireplace in her most dignified manner. Sarah watched in awe as her sister, looking magnificent in her black grenadine dress with its pale green trim, calmly explained. Many women would have crumbled in such circumstances, but not her Miriam. "So you see that it is all an unfortunate mistake," she concluded.

Mr. Garie did not seem amused, but was polite. "Well, Miss Morgan, he secured the marriage license this afternoon. However, when you stand and I ask if you will take Mr. Carter as your husband, it is your privilege to answer 'No.'"

Miriam frowned. "That would be a mockery, sir. Our wager was in jest. Will knew that, and it must go no farther."

Before she finished, a rapid step was heard in the back hall. Then Will's voice calling. "Where is she?"

Fear gripped Sarah as she sat powerless in the chair. Reckless Will had almost shot Miriam once while playing with his pistol. What might he be capable of in a rage? Sarah could imagine the bone-chilling twenty-mile ride he had just made from his home in Clinton. Surely he had urged his tired horse with whip and spur, thinking, "She's mine at last!"

"Frank, help me save her!" cried Sarah.

Frank shushed her. "I'll do my best if you will only keep still and not hurt yourself."

Then Gibbes appeared, taking Miriam's arm with his unbandaged one and propelling her upstairs. The slamming of a door told them the bride was caged. Sarah gripped the arms of her chair as Will Carter strode into the room, his boots heavy on the hard cypress floor. His cheeks were flushed and his silk cravat crooked from the frenzied ride. It was obvious that he had dressed in his best suit, his wedding suit. For a moment, his labored breathing and the fire's crackle were the only sounds in the parlor. Triumphantly, he threw the license on the table. "Where is Miriam?" he demanded.

Everyone began talking at once, trying to explain, to calm him. "It is folly, Will. You can't force her to marry you," they said. "She is not coming down."

As the truth finally sank in, he collapsed in agony too great for tears. "Miriam, Miriam!" he moaned. "She cannot be so cruel. Surely she will take pity on me. Call her now!"

But Miriam was not allowed to come, and the brokenhearted man eventually rode away. Sarah was carried up to the bedroom she shared with Miriam, where they lay awake most of the night. Miriam felt wretched and yet, just as the room grew quiet, would start up with a fresh shriek of laughter. Sarah would pinch and subdue her with, "Think of poor Will. Think of what Mother and Lilly are going through in Clinton, where everyone thinks you are married by now."

Miriam sobered. "It will certainly do Mother's health no good. Tomorrow I will take the cars up to Clinton and tell her the truth myself."

Temporarily satisfied, Sarah drifted off to sleep.

The next day was Sunday. Miriam went to Clinton and the others to church, leaving Sarah alone to catch up on her diary. There was so much to record. She lay face down, struggling with a spattering pen and clotted ink, when a step was heard on the stair. *What if it should be Will?* she asked herself, then shook her head at the thought.

The steps came nearer. Sarah raised her head to meet a ghastly smile. "Will!"

"Sarah!" he exclaimed, stepping forward to grip her outstretched hand. She had never seen a more heartbroken, wobegone man.

"Where is my bride?" he asked, forcing a laugh. "Pshaw! I know she has gone to Clinton. I have come to talk to *you*. Wasn't it a merry wedding?"

"Sit down and let me talk," Sarah said gently.

So he did. Sarah tried to hide her nervousness,

for she knew so little about dealing with wild natures. Yet, he must be calmed, must give up that marriage license before it caused further grief. If Miriam's name remained on record as Mrs. Carter, their brothers would sooner or later get involved. "You have compromised her name, Will," Sarah reminded him. "If you profess to love her, why would you do her such a wrong?"

His eyes blazed. *"Profess?* You know I adore her!"

"Very well. This girl you love then, you mean to make miserable. Is this love?"

"Do you really think my keeping the license affects her reputation?" he asked, as if the thought had not occurred to him.

"Ask yourself! Is it right that you hold in your hands the evidence that she is Mrs. Carter, when she is not and never will be? Is it honorable?"

Will buried his face in his hands. "I have loved Miriam for the past three years. I'd rather die than grieve her, or never see her again."

Sarah knew that she had touched the right key, and allowed him to ramble on. Finally admitting that he knew Miriam had wagered herself in jest, he agreed to deliver the license and have the record cleared. With swimming eyes, he rose to leave. "You are hard on me, Sarah. I could have made her happy, I know, because I worship her so. Why are you against me? But God bless you! Goodbye!" Then he was gone.

"Why?" Sarah whispered to the open door. "Oh Will, because I love my sister too much to see her miserable merely to make you happy!"

Christmas came quickly. In honor of the day, Sarah was carried downstairs and wheeled to the long dining table. She had not seen one in so many weeks that she hardly tasted the food for the novelty of so many faces. Miriam wore the new collar and cuffs Dellie had crocheted for her and Lilly had sent on the cars. Sarah had a set as well, from little Morgan. *How typical of Lilly to prompt them to do such a sweet thing,* thought Sarah. *I don't believe she ever thinks of herself, but if we were a thousand miles away she would never rest until she had sent some token of the day. And what did I ever do for her?* Sarah could think of nothing.

Though there were no carolers this year, Colonel Breaux had sent a band from Port Hudson to serenade the family the night before. General Carter invited some of the other officers to join them, so Linwood was filled with company and good cheer. After dinner there was a rap on the door and Santa Claus himself was admitted, to their great surprise. The jolly fellow wore an old uniform of the Mexican War and a preposterous beard of short, tangled curls. He carried a basket from which he drew a gift. Pausing before each lady, he would bow and present her with a small cake; the gentlemen received a wine glass replenished from a mysterious black bottle. Then, leaving them all with wonder and laughter, he retired with a much lighter basket.

January 1st. Thursday. 1863.

1863! Why I have hardly become accustomed to writing '62 yet! Where has the year gone? With all its troubles and anxieties, it is the shortest I ever spent. '61 & '62 together would hardly seem 365 days to me. Well, let time fly. Every hour brings us nearer our freedom, and we are two years nearer peace now, than we were when South Carolina first seceded.

We had a merry time watching the old year out. O didn't Mr. Halsey send me the most beautiful white Camelia for my New Year's gift! What is it I love better than flowers? Not human beings, certainly! I would not let it go down stairs; I kept it up here where I could look at it all the time. I believe I love God better when I see flowers; this one looks as though He had not yet taken his finger off it.

Sunday January 4th. Sis' birthday.

One just from Baton Rouge tells us that a Yankee colonel and his wife inhabit our house. They say they look strangely at home on our front gallery, pacing up and down as though at home. O my garden! Do they respect you? And a stranger and a Yankee occupies our father's place at the table. The table that has been surrounded by his children and friends for so long, the table sacred to our pleasant dinners. And the old lamp that shone in the parlor the night I was born, that with its great beaming eye watched us one by one as we grew up and left our homes; that witnessed every parting and meeting, by which we sang, read, talked, danced and made merry. Our old lamp has passed into the hands of strangers who neither know nor care for its history. And mother's bed belongs now to a Yankee woman!

Mid-January brought a more pleasant surprise. After months of prayers and frequent news of his exploits, Will Pinkney came to visit. Though Will was discouraged with the war, his little son was fine, and his wife enjoyed Sarah's letters almost as much as he did. Talking with her old friend brought back memories of happier times, and Sarah was sorry when at twilight he arose to leave.

"You will be well soon, I know," Will said. "If your doctor cared as much for you as I do, he would tie you in bed and force you to be careful."

"Just as though I am not!" Sarah retorted. "No, I will never be well again. My life is told."

"You *shall* get well!" he argued. "Remember how you used to like to waltz with me? We'll have many a glorious dance yet!"

Sarah smiled, grateful for the encouragement. "Not unless you engage me for the first quadrille in Heaven, Will—I'll never dance on earth again."

The following week brought Sarah to the end of her third diary. She was desolate, for writing had become her chief occupation during the cold days and long winter nights. Two months had passed since the accident, and her mother had arranged for their family doctor from Baton Rouge to examine her. It was good to again see Dr. Woods, whose sympathy was touching. "You will recover, to a certain extent; but will feel it more or less all your life," he told her.

Sarah decided that if this were true, she could accept it as God's will and refuse to complain to those around her. But inwardly she fumed over the painful and ineffective treatments her previous doctors had ordered. When someone procured a new diary for her, what a relief it was to tell *someone.*

> *Thursday 22d Jan.*
>
> *Well! What is written will come to pass. First comes a Doctor with a butchering apparatus who cups and bleeds me unmercifully, says I'll walk ten days after, and exit.*
>
> *Enter another. Croton oil and strychnine pills. That'll set me up in two weeks, and exit.*
>
> *Enter a third. Sounds my bones and pinches them from my head to my heels. Tells of the probability of a splinter of bone knocked off my left hip, the possibility of paralysis in the leg, the certainty of a seriously injured spine, and the necessity for the most violent counter irritants. Follows blisters which sicken even disinterested people to look at.*
>
> *Enter the fourth. Inhuman butchery! Wonder they did not kill you! Take three drops a day out of this tiny bottle, and presto! In two weeks you are walking!*

A fifth, in the character of a friend, says, "My dear young lady, if you do, your case is hopeless. What wonder that I am puzzled? I want to believe all, but how is it possible? Of this I am satisfied: if Dr. Woods thought me beyond his skills, he has too much regard for me to trifle with my life.

Having vented her frustrations, Sarah turned her attention to other matters. Knowing that each day brought Federal forces nearer Port Hudson and his beloved Linwood was in greater peril, General Carter was doing an unheard of thing—he was giving a party!

The household bustled with preparations as Miriam and Anna made sure that every young man in whom they had the least bit of interest was invited. Guests began arriving early on the cars that day. Sarah enjoyed the company, yet knew for the first time in her life she would be forced to watch the dance without participating. With the dreadful pain fastened into her back like shark's teeth, she watched the girls dress. In her haste to assemble the perfect outfit, Miriam practically buried Sarah under cast-off skirts, cards, and dresses. And impatience did not improve the temper of young Anna, who slapped her little maid Malvina in the excitement.

When they had dressed, Miriam remembered Sarah, practically hidden beneath the bed full of clothes. "I wish you would reconsider coming down with us," she said.

Sarah shook her head, trying to keep her voice

pleasant. "You both look beautiful. Go dance a quadrille for me."

When they were gone, Malvina came to rescue Sarah from the chaotic mass of clothing. Sarah lay quietly, fighting the tears that threatened to spill down her cheeks. She and Malvina should have sympathized with each other. Malvina would have broken her neck for Sarah, while she would rather disobey Anna than eat her dinner. Yet both were silent as the bed was cleared and the music started downstairs.

Sarah finally cleared her throat and spoke. "Thank you, Malvina. Would you help me get dressed now?"

Malvina looked puzzled, then nodded. "Sure, Miss Sarah. What would you like to wear to the party?"

Since it was impossible to wear a full dress, Sarah chose the morning dress that she had received the most compliments on. It was pale blue with embroidered skirt, rich lace trim, and handkerchief to match. Adding a jet black bracelet and tiny blue bow to her braided hair, she decided not to consult the mirror again. It was useless to compete with the other girls. She would not even try.

Frank Enders was asked to carry her downstairs, for his strong back and steady arms made the precarious journey less frightening than with others who had tried it. Soon Sarah was settled in her chair, the long folds of her skirt hiding its wheels.

Several friends teased by asking her to dance, and she tried to decline in a lighthearted way.

Then a strange gentleman bowed and asked for the next dance. Realizing that he was serious, Sarah explained, "I am sorry, sir, but am compelled by an unfortunate accident to play the invalid at present."

The man's ferocious mustache twitched. "Oh, I didn't realize . . . Please accept my apology, miss."

"Of course," Sarah said. "I thought everyone knew."

The fellow excused himself and spent the next five minutes making inquiries about her. Sarah made her own and was startled to learn that the stout, very handsome man in the sailorish costume was none other than Col. Robert Crockett, son of the famed Davy Crockett. She had heard of him since his arrival at Port Hudson—a wild, reckless type that she would normally avoid. Yet the gentleman who returned to spend part of his evening with her was among the most charming and compassionate she had met.

As Sarah watched the dancers, she was glad that she had come down. Linwood's walls resounded with laughter, tinkling spurs, and music of the polka, two-step, and waltz. Then, at midnight, the General came to move her, and Sarah was afraid that she would be sent to bed. However, it was only supper time. Instead, she was wheeled out to the back gallery which had been enclosed with curtains. A beautiful table was set with a meal that caused all to marvel. Where had the Carters found such food in these days of scarcity? Thirty-five happy faces surrounded the table for the best meal they had enjoyed in a long while.

It was five o'clock the next morning when the guests finally retired. "What a heathenish, indecent hour!" one of the girls remarked, laughing as they went upstairs. Sarah only wished that it could have gone on forever.

Chapter 17

❖

Bombardment

Monday Feb. 9th 1863 Night

A letter from my dear little Jimmy! How glad I am, words could not express. This is the first since he arrived in England, and now we know what has become of him at last. While awaiting the completion of the iron clad gunboat to which he has been appointed, he has put himself to school, and studies hard. How he raves about the Yankees! What bloody vengence he swears on them for the destruction of our home. I had to laugh at his intense hatred. Better to leave them to God and their own conscience. Remorse would be torture enough, if they happen to be honest men.

My delight at hearing from Jimmy is overcast by the bad news Lilly sends of Mother's health. Her health has been wretched for three months. I was never separated from Mother so long before; and I am home sick, and heart sick about her. Only twenty miles apart, and she with a shocking bone felon in her hand and that dreadful cough, unable to come to me, whilst I am lying helpless here, as unable to get to her. My poor Mother! She will die if she stays in Clinton. I cant stand this. I must get to her by some means.

Sunday Feb. 15th. 1863

Late in the evening Will Pinkney came to see me. I was myself again, and with him and Miriam sitting by my bed, spent a delightful evening. I was glad to see a gleam of his old self appear . . .

Wednesday Feb. 18th.

Gibbes has gone back to his regiment. I cant say how dreary I felt when he came to tell me good bye. I did not mean to cry; but how could I help it when he put his arms around me and sobbed so bitterly. Gibbes loves his little sister. Dear brother, I have never deserved it! But he cried like a child—as though we were never to meet again; and I cried too, just because I knew what he was thinking. The tears of forty thousand women would not affect me as much as the single sob of a man. May heaven spare me the frequent repetition of the sight!

Sunday Feb. 22d. 1863

Mother has come to me! O how glad I was to see her this morning. And the Georgia project is a reality—yes! Shall we really go? Will some page in this book actually record "Augusta, Georgia?"

No, I dare not believe it. Yet the mere thought has given me strength within the last two weeks to attempt to walk. Learning to walk at my age! Is it not amusing? But the smallest baby knows more than I did at first. Of course I knew one foot was to be put before the other; but the question was how it was to be done, when they would not go? I have conquered the difficulty however, and can now

*walk almost two yards, if someone holds me fast.
But O my unspeakable horror of walking alone!*

*Sunset. Will Pinkney has this instant left. Ever
since dinner he has been vehemently opposing the
Georgia move, insisting that it will cost me my life, by
rendering me a confirmed cripple. I am afraid his
arguments have about shaken Mother's resolution.*

Monday Feb. 23d.

*Here goes! News has been received that the
Yankees are already packed, ready to march
against us at any hour. Hope amounts to pre-
sumption at Port Hudson. They are confident that
our fifteen thousand can repulse twice the number. Great God! —I say it with all reverence—if we
could defeat them! My heart beats but one
prayer—Victory! Victory!*

*In the mean time though, Linwood is in danger.
This dear place, my second home; its loved inhabitants; think of their being in such peril. But I must
leave before. No use of leaving my bones for the
Yankees to pick.*

March came with its white dogwood scattered
through the woods, purple splashes of azalea, and
wisteria perfume. However, the beauty of spring
was lost on the inhabitants of Linwood as they prepared to flee. Mother's news of shortages in
Clinton was alarming—many days they had only
hominy to eat. Poor Lilly had started putting her
children to bed early to make them forget they
were hungry.

Before Mother returned, Sarah and Miriam persuaded one of the Carter servants to sell them a

chicken and basket of eggs to send with her. Food was growing scarce at Linwood as well. In weaker moments the girls would speculate on what they missed most—Lydia wished for an oyster, Anna craved roast chicken, Miriam wanted fruit, and Sarah thought a cup of coffee and piece of wheat bread would be the greatest treats in the world.

The girls began to pack. Sarah pulled out her old running bag as Miriam piled her other belongings on the bed.

"This bustle and confusion reminds me of our last days in Baton Rouge," said Miriam.

"With one exception," said Sarah. "How am I to run this time?"

"Well, the steps you have taken are encouraging."

Sarah nodded. "It will require many more steps to take us wherever we are to land."

"True. I only wish we knew where Mother will decide to go—Augusta or to Brother's in New Orleans. This uncertainty is killing me," Miriam complained.

"I hope Gibbes can find us accommodations in Georgia. I hate the thought of going back into Federal territory, even if we have family in New Orleans. They might even make us take that despicable oath of allegiance. And how could we see Gibbes again, or any of the boys, until the war is over?"

Miriam sighed. "The only way our friends could enter New Orleans would be as prisoners of war.

They are being kept in the Customs House, you know."

Sarah continued to pack.

Saturday March 14th. 5 o'clock P.M.

They are coming! The Yankees are coming at last! For four or five hours the sound of their cannon has assailed our ears. There! That one shook my bed! O they are coming! God spare our brave soldiers, and lead them to victory!

They are now within four miles of us, on the big road to Baton Rouge. Only we seven women remain in the house. The General left this morning, to our unspeakable relief. They would hang him, we fear, if they should find him here. If they will burn the house, they will have to burn me in it. For I cannot walk, and I know they shall not carry me. I write, touch my guitar, talk, pick lint, and pray so rapidly that it is hard to say which is my occupation.

Half past One o'clock A.M. It has come at last! What an awful sound! I thought I had heard a bombardment before; but Baton Rouge's experience was child's play compared to this. At half past eleven came the first gun. Instantly I had my hand on Miriam, and at my first exclamation, Mrs. Badger and Anna answered. All three sprang to their feet to dress, while all four of us prayed aloud.

Such an incessant roar! At every report the house shaking so, and we thinking of our dear soldiers. That dreadful roar! I cant think fast enough. They are too quick to be counted. We have all been in Mrs. Carter's room, from the last window of which we can see the incessant flash of the guns, and the great shooting stars of flame. There is a burning house in the distance, the second one we have seen to night.

Gathered in a knot, we women up here watched in the faint star light the flashes from the guns, and silently wondered which of our friends were lying stiff and dead, and then shuddering at the thought, betook our selves to silent prayer. I think we know what it is to "wrestle with God in prayer."

Firing has slackened considerably. We know absolutely nothing; when does one ever know anything in the country? But we presume that this is an engagement between our batteries and the gunboats attempting to run the blockade. All are to lie down already dressed. I shall go to sleep, though we may expect at any instant to hear the tramp of Yankee cavalry in the yard.

Chapter 18

❖

Night Crossing

The next morning, to her great surprise, Sarah woke to find herself still alive. For a moment she wondered if there had really been a bombardment the night before or if she had written a dream. The other women settled her mind about that.

"Did you hear that last explosion, just before dawn?" Mrs. Badger asked.

"No."

"Amazing," said the older woman. "It was the most terrific noise I have ever heard."

As the day progressed, news came from Port Hudson. The night's battle had started when several Yankee gunboats were fired upon by Confederate batteries placed on bluffs overlooking the river. One was sunk, while another old sidewheeler, the *Mississippi,* ran aground and was abandoned. When fire caused her to explode, the sound was heard fifty miles away. The two boats that succeeded in passing the batteries were also damaged.

To the surprise of all, Yankee soldiers did not appear. Instead it was reported that their land forces had withdrawn to Baton Rouge. The girls were relieved to have General Carter home and to learn that none of their friends or family members had been harmed. Passes were limited and visits from the officers less frequent, for the enemy was sure to return. The greatest concern was that it would be a long campaign designed to starve well-fortified Port Hudson into surrender.

Sarah's brother in New Orleans continued to smuggle letters out to Mother, begging them to come. When Gibbes wrote that it was impossible to find a vacant room in Augusta, her decision was made.

"Oh, I don't, don't want to go!" cried Sarah. "If only we could find a resting place in the Confederacy."

"Mother has written everywhere. It is impossible," said Miriam. "Sarah, she will die in Clinton. The hardship is too great for her health. And the medicines you need are no longer available here. It must be New Orleans."

"Our friends here will think we are traitors," Sarah argued. "I cannot bear that."

"That is ridiculous. Everyone understands and wants what is best for us." Miriam pointed to the leg Sarah was pulling a stocking on. "Look how thin you have become. There is no obstacle from your ankle to your knee."

Sarah could not argue with that. Making a wry face, she felt her leg. "If I were a cow I would certainly go dry, for I have lost my calf."

Miriam laughed loudly. "And your bones have

grown completely immodest. See how they stand out with so little flesh to cover them."

Sarah sighed. Perhaps it was time for a change.

When the news was announced that they were leaving, several friends, including Frank Enders, stopped to say goodbye. "You must kiss me good-bye this time, Sarah," he told her.

"I will see about it," she said, putting him off. Actually she had put everyone off until now, insisting that her first kiss should be for her husband, if she should ever have one.

"Fine," he said. "I shall speak to your mother about it."

Which he did. To Sarah's unspeakable surprise, Mother said, "Certainly!"

As Frank returned to claim his kiss, Sarah realized she had carried the joke too far. "Oh, wait awhile. Let me kiss the General first, then *maybe* I will kiss you."

General Carter kissed Sarah's cheek and Frank advanced again.

"Wait!" she cried, throwing up a hand. "Kiss Miriam first."

Acting like a sensible girl, Miriam casually threw back her veil and kissed Frank as though he were one of her brothers. He turned back. "Now, Miss Sarah!"

As Frank drew nearer, Sarah remembered a remark he had once made about wanting to kiss her more that any girl he knew, because it was a liberty no other man would take. She took a deep breath. As much as she liked Frank, her principles would not be compromised to satisfy his pride. He was six inches from her face when she stopped him. "Oh, Frank! Don't, please!"

He drew back, looking mortified.

"Kiss him, you silly thing and be done with it!" cried the General.

"Sarah, you are absurd," lectured Miriam.

Mother shocked her again by taking Frank's side. "Sarah, you are behaving badly. Kiss Frank this instant! You might as well object to kissing your brother!"

What? Let Frank think he can do what no one else dared? Never! thought Sarah. Ignoring the scolding, she stuck out her hand. "I can't kiss you, Frank, and am more than sorry I jested about it. Let us part friends."

He finally accepted the hand and shook it heartily. When they were on the train, Sarah and Miriam continued to debate the subject of kissing. "I was right," Sarah insisted. "No woman has a right to kiss a man she does not intend to marry, even if they are engaged. What if the engagement is broken off ? How would it feel to meet the dear boy who has enjoyed so many kisses?"

"You are a torment, Sarah."

"No! I have nothing to give the man I marry except a pure heart. So I keep myself pure from the world, kisses, and other quicksands—there is no knowing where the next step will take you. When the marriage ceremony is over, I want to be able to say to my dear Whomever, 'Here is a mouth, not pretty to be sure, but yours will be the first lips that ever touched it.' And if he is not charmed with the gift, I shall say he is a brute and unworthy of the trouble I have taken in preserving his future treasure."

Wednesday, Clinton. April 8th 1863.

Our last adieux are said, and Linwood is left behind, "it may be for years, and it may be forever." I grew almost lachrymose as I bid a last adieu to the bed where I have spent so many months, as they carried me down stairs. Wonder if it will miss me?

Mrs. Carter grew quite pathetic as the cars approached, while poor Lydia clung first to Miriam and then to me, as though we parted to meet only in eternity. Anna went through her last adieux with such a woe begone face and damp cheeks, that I really feared I should catch cold from the shower bath. Mrs. Badger had great red rims like crimson spectacles around her eyes as she kissed me good bye. Seems to me she should have been glad to be rid of the constant care and trouble I had given her ever since I was injured. Bless her dear kind heart! How good she has been to me!

The cars gave a whistle, a jerk and we were off. I put my head out to see the women using their handkerchiefs to wipe tears and wave farewell, while the General waved his hat for good bye. And my last view of Frank showed him waving his handkerchief, where upon I kissed my hand to him. Good bye Frank! Sorry I hurt your feelings, but am satisfied you think none the less of me. I have retained your respect, as well as my own.

Then green hedges rapidly changing took their place, and Linwood was out of sight, before we had ceased saying, "God bless the kind hearts we left behind."

What a delightful sensation is motion, after five months' inaction. To see green trees and wild flowers once more after such an illness, is a pleasure that only those long deprived of such beauties can fully appreciate.

At their stop in Clinton, Sarah was delighted to find that Lilly's children had not forgotten her. "Aunt Sarah!" they cried as ten little arms threatened to squeeze the breath from her. There was little sleep that night as Lilly grieved over not knowing when she would see them again; however, while Charlie fought for the Confederacy, she would not leave it.

The next morning found Sarah settled on pillows for the train ride to Camp Moore. It was pleasant, though tiring, and that night she was grateful for the comfortable bed that wrapped around her weary bones. But the best feature of the home in which they boarded was the food—wheat bread, loaf sugar, preserves, and coffee! Not the potato, burnt sugar, and parched corn abomination, but real coffee beans.

Thus fortified, they journeyed on to Hammond, a train stop boasting about four houses. Sarah was basically enjoying the trip, except for her need to be lifted in and out of conveyances. Being carried by complete strangers caused her to blush more than once.

A long carriage ride the following day brought Sarah, Miriam, Mother, and Tiche to Madisonville, a half-deserted village on the Tchefuncte River. A boarding house owned by a Mrs. Greyson was to be their home until passports arrived from New Orleans. Mother had written the Yankee commander, General Pemberton, requesting permission to enter for health reasons. There had been no reply, though some said that a note from Confederate General Gardner would do. Before leaving Clinton she had secured one, hoping it would help. The officials at Madisonville were not impressed.

Two other ladies in the house, Mrs. Bull and Mrs. Ivy, also waited for passes from New Orleans. Meanwhile Mrs. Greyson worked hard to make their stay pleasant. Strawberries were in season, and the guests were well supplied with fresh berries and cream. Sarah thought she would never get enough, and only wished that Lilly's brood could share them. Mrs. Greyson also invited some of the local soldiers to call on her guests. They were more rustic than the men Sarah knew from Baton Rouge, but came armed with flower bouquets and a banjo for entertainment.

As pleasant as their stay was, Mother still suffered with her hand, and their rooms cost four dollars per day. Mrs. Ivy with her two sick babies was also anxious to get home. Soon Mrs. Bull suggested a new plan to leave immediately for a plantation called Bonfouca, thirty miles away, where schooners called twice a week from New Orleans. It was said that they would allow passengers without a pass. Carriages were waiting on the other side of the river.

"We will leave immediately," Mother declared.

As everyone packed in haste, Mrs. Greyson sniffed their many bouquets of flowers. "I believe you have made the right decision, though I shall be sorry to lose the company of the young ladies," she told Mother. "They are such comforts, and somehow the flowers all seem to follow them."

Two hours later the group of five ladies, four small children, and four servants climbed into a large scow to cross the Tchefuncte. Half a mile downstream they found the carriages waiting, and journeyed on until they reached Lake Ponchartrain. Staring at the great expanse of water, Sarah suddenly felt lonely, desolate. Once across, she would no longer be a part of the Confederacy.

The driver suggested a local couple who might board them for the night. It turned out that they lived in a small Acadian cottage and spoke only French. When they discovered Sarah's condition, she was given the best room in the house, which included a narrow single bed and a pine armoir filled with dried corn. She was also given the only mosquito bar in the house, which she insisted on sharing. Supper consisted of an egg and a spoonful of rice. There was no breakfast.

The next leg of their journey wound through twenty-three miles of piney woods to the plantation called Bonfouca. It seemed much longer because the horse refused to move unless Miriam drove and the driver ran alongside. Bonfouca's overseer greeted them with distressing news.

"You cannot stop here, madam," he informed them. "I am sorry, but you must go back."

The passengers in the Morgan carriage exploded in anger. "Go back? When we are almost at journey's end and our money nearly spent? After these long miles and fatigue?" Sarah cried.

"With my sick babies!" cried Mrs. Ivy.

"With my sick child!" cried Sarah's mother. "Never! You may turn us out, but we will die in the woods first! To go back is to kill my daughter and these babies!"

"Madam, I have orders to allow no one to pass who has not written permission. I am liable to imprisonment if I harbor those who have no passport," the man explained.

"But we have General Gardner's order," Sarah protested.

"Then you shall certainly pass. But these ladies cannot," he added, indicating Mrs. Bull and Mrs. Ivy.

The sympathetic man finally relented and showed them all to a large, unfurnished house. Mrs. Bull sat in a calm, dignified state of despair, while young Mrs. Ivy dissolved in tears. Sarah, Miriam, and their mother were equally concerned, for their common troubles had formed a bond. The night that followed was long and uncomfortable. There were not enough mattresses and bed clothes to go around. One of Miriam's dresses acted as mosquito bar to protect them from the flying marauders.

The next day was spent waiting for the schooner. By evening, when they had almost despaired of its coming, a sail was sighted coming up the bayou, also called Bonfouca. They had hardly gone below deck before Sarah wished herself back on land. The entire cabin was the size of her bed back home, with a mattress only two feet wide.

Just before midnight, the schooner weighed anchor and began its journey across Lake Ponchartrain. The passengers went on deck for a last look at Dixie. Every heart was full. Each woman left brothers, sisters, husband, children, or dear friends behind. Looking at the beautiful starlight shining on the last boundary of their glorious land, they sang, "Farewell, Dear Land" with quavering voices. Then fervently, silently praying, they passed from its sight. *God bless you, all you dear ones we have left in our beloved country! God bless and prosper you, and grant you victory in the name of Jesus Christ.*

———— ❖ ————

The schooner had not sailed far when the stars vanished behind dark, threatening clouds. "It'll be a very ugly night on the lake," the captain announced, shaking his head.

"It's because of that corpse we're carrying," said one of the sailors. "Bad luck."

Sarah's heart went to her throat as the other passengers grew alarmed.

"What corpse?" someone asked.

"There's a lady taking a body home for burial," the captain explained.

"We'll founder for sure," came another discomforting remark.

While other sailors' superstitions were discussed, Sarah returned to her cabin and tried to rest. It was impossible. The boat's rocking made Mrs. Ivy's babies ill and they spent the rest of the night shrieking, kicking, crying, throwing up, and going through the whole list of infant performances. When the noise and odor became unbearable, Sarah staggered back on deck. She found Miriam there and, fortunately, no storm. The only wind was a damp head-breeze. Miriam helped Sarah to a bench and covered her with shawls until daylight.

When land was sighted, there was a general smoothing of hair and dresses.

"They will inspect our luggage before allowing us through," Mrs. Bull told the Morgans.

Sarah remembered her diary and knew what she must do. Digging it out, she passed a piece of tape through the center. "Miriam, raise your skirts a minute."

Miriam looked at her oddly. "Why?"

"To tie this under your hoops. The Yankees must not see it."

With a sigh and a shake of her head, Miriam fastened the diary securely. "Satisfied?"

Sarah nodded. Soon they entered the canal that led to Hickok's Landing, and Federal territory. All around stood men in the dark blue uniforms she had not seen in many months. Sarah had not missed them. The women stood together, trying not to let their nervousness show.

Finally they landed. Two officers met them, asking for passports.

"We have none," the ladies said in unison.

Another officer came. "Have any of you taken the oath?"

None of the passengers had taken the oath of allegiance to the United States. He wrote down their names—all except Sarah's mother, who had stayed in her cabin.

"This vessel had fifteen passengers, but I have only fourteen names," said the officer.

Mother was called, gave her name, and disappeared again. Sarah grew uneasy, knowing that her mother was preparing for a scene. Her worries were interrupted by a young man kneeling to examine their baggage. She had to smile at the respectful way he handled the girls' dirty petticoats and stockings.

"Of course, the Confederates have already searched this," he said.

"Indeed they did not touch it!" said Sarah. "They never think of doing such work."

The unfortunate young man's cheeks turned red. "Miss, it is more mortifying to me than it can be to you."

When the baggage had passed inspection, another officer came to administer the despised Eagle oath. First he called roll.

"Sarah Morgan!"

"Here," she said quietly.

"Stand up!"

"I cannot."

"Why not?"

Sarah raised her chin. "Unable," she said firmly.

He went on until all were standing but Sarah, then passed out strips of paper with each person's name, stating that they had taken the oath as citizens of the United States. She rejoiced inside, thinking they were finished. Then the man removed his hat and told everyone to raise their right hands.

Sarah cleared her throat. "I do not wish to take this oath, sir. Is there any other way?"

"None whatever!" he barked. "You have to do it, and there is no getting out of it."

Struggling not to cry, Sarah half-covered her face with her raised hand and started to pray. She prayed so hard for her brothers and the Confederacy that she heard only her own voice. The man's recitation was simply noise that she refused to listen to, until the question struck her ear, "So help you God?"

Sarah shuddered and prayed harder. There was an awful pause in which not a lip moved. Then the soldier threw down his black book and declared, "All right!" The nightmare was over.

Sarah sat frozen. The process of becoming Yankee had brought no nasty or disagreeable feeling. She would pray as hard as ever for the boys and *her* country.

The soldier went to the tiny cabin's entrance and

called to Mother. "Mrs. Morgan, are you ready to take the oath?"

Mother climbed the ladder with all dignity she could muster, using her one good hand. "I suppose I *have* to, since I belong to you."

"No, madam, you are not obliged; we force no one. Can you state your objections?"

It was the wrong question to ask Mother. Dizzy with hunger and sleeplessness, frustrated and in pain, she felt her nerves were beyond control. "Yes, I have three sons fighting against you, and you have robbed me, beggared me!" she cried, launching into a speech in which the Yankees were blamed for every misfortune of the past two years, right down to her sore hand.

Miriam, Mrs. Bull, and Mrs. Ivy begged her to stop. Sarah did not try, for at such moments Mother was to be controlled by no one but Father and Brother—Father was gone and their brother, Judge Philip Morgan, had not yet arrived.

The officer was losing patience. "Madam, I did not invite you to come," he said briskly. Then ordering several more soldiers on board, he allowed the boat to continue up the canal to the city.

Mother returned to her cabin in tears as the rest waited for whatever was to come. When they reached the landing in New Orleans, Miriam immediately sent a note to Brother's home.

The hot noonday sun was glaring off the water before the officers returned. Sarah felt herself growing weaker from the heat, hunger, and a sleepless night. Alarmed by her appearance, Mrs. Bull begged an officer to let Sarah off the boat.

"No, madam. It is impossible," said the officer. "We have orders to wait until General Bowens comes."

"But this young lady has been ill for months; she is perfectly exhausted, and will faint if she is not removed at once," pleaded Mrs. Bull.

"Those are the orders," the officer said stubbornly.

Mrs. Bull would not give up. "Do you think you are performing your duty as a gentleman and a Christian? This young lady has obtained her pass already, without the slightest difficulty."

The officer shook his head, repeating his orders.

"Then allow me to take her to her brother while the others remain here. You will have the rest of the family and their trunk as hostages."

The man wavered, then nodded in agreement. Sarah could wait in the office.

Sarah was growing so faint and deathly sick that she didn't know where they were guiding her, and didn't care. Nor did she remember saying goodbye to Mrs. Bull and Mrs. Ivy. A man's voice said something about arrests, but the ringing in her ears drowned his words, and instead of his face there were whirling carriage wheels . . . and Brother.

Sunday April 26th. New Orleans.

I am getting well! Bless the Lord O my soul! Life, health, and happiness dawn on my trembling view again! Is not this delight worth the five months and a half of suspense and pain? Yes! I am getting well!

On Thursday, a day to be marked with a white

stone in my memory, for the first time since the eleventh of November I discarded my nightgown, put on a dress and—walked to breakfast! And better still, scorning the bed that has been my best friend through all these long months, I adopted this easy chair instead.

Dr. Stone came a few hours after I arrived; this morning I walked out to meet him and he asked how my sister was! When I assured him I was myself, he exclaimed, "God bless my soul! You don't say so!" evidently astonished at the resurrection. He attributes it to Belladonna and gentle exercise; I say thank God and dont care to know why or wherefore.

I wonder why I could never keep a respectable diary? I have tried to look back here and there, to find one redeeming touch, one description as interesting or amusing as the original, but have been forced to relinquish the search from sheer disgust. I am strongly tempted to throw it in the fire every time I look at it. There is but one thing that withholds me; and that is the fact of its being the work of my sick hours. Written for the most part while suffering severely, and fighting desperately against blank despair, I may as well keep it to remember the dark hours when pen and ink proved my best friends. One should not forget tried friends.

Then I'll keep this as a souvenir of my dark days—those days when Hope threatened to unfold her wings and leave me a cripple on this fair earth, and I struggled boldly to make the world believe she had not gone yet, and did not mean to.

Conclusion

Although Sarah was safe in her brother's home, the war was not yet over for her. As Port Hudson endured the longest siege in American military history (forty-eight days), the Morgans prayed earnestly for their friends and relatives. Union forces invaded Linwood, converting it into a hospital. After Vicksburg's surrender on July 4, General Gardner realized that Port Hudson's situation was hopeless. On July 9, 1863, it, too, surrendered. Enlisted men were released while officers, some of them friends of the family, were brought to the New Orleans prison. Miriam later married one of them, Lt. Alcee Dupre.

In February of the next year, the family was devastated to learn that both Gibbes and George had died in military hospitals. Jimmy survived, however, and married soon after the war ended in 1865. Sarah and her mother then moved to South Carolina to be near him.

It was there that Sarah finally met her "perfect man." Francis Warrington Dawson, a friend of Jimmy, had left his home in England to fight for the Confederacy. After the war he became editor of a Charleston newspaper. Although journalism was considered a man's profession, Frank Dawson invited Sarah to write a series of articles for the paper on women's issues. They married in 1874 and had two children, Ethel and Warrington.

After Frank's death, Sarah eventually moved to Paris where Warrington worked as a writer and diplomat. In 1903 she published *Les Aventures de Jeannot Lap,* a French version of the Br'er Rabbit stories which was adopted as a textbook in France. She died in Paris at the age of sixty-seven, leaving her diary to the son who had begged her not to burn it. At the end she wrote:

Reading this for the first time, in all these many years, I wish to bear record that God never failed me, through stranger vicissitudes than I ever dared record. Whatever the anguish, whatever the extremity, in His own good time He ever delivered me. So that I bless Him to-day for all of life's joys and sorrows—for all He gave—for all He has taken—and I bear witness that it was all Very Good.

Sarah Morgan Dawson.
July 23rd, 1896.
Charleston,
South Carolina

Author's Note

❖

I am most grateful to Sarah Morgan's son, Warrington Dawson, for not allowing her diary to be destroyed. Perhaps she felt it was too personal to share, but the thoughts and feelings so clearly drawn are the ingredients that make this the truest, most human form of history.

In 1913 Dawson published about half the material as *A Confederate Girl's Diary*. In 1960 Indiana University Press published a Civil War centennial edition, adding material by James I. Robertson, Jr. A complete transcription of the diary was published in 1991 by Charles East and the University of Georgia Press. East's patient, meticulous work with the microfilm, loaned from Duke University, is impressive, indeed.

I first became acquainted with Sarah Morgan while researching the Civil War in south Louisiana. It seemed that I had lived in her hometown for thirty years and had traveled the same roads, yet never knowing about Sarah, or of Baton Rouge's role in the Civil War. Since I was already writing for young people, it was my desire to make her story more accessible to them. While this version is novelized for easier reading, and liberties have been taken with some scenes, about 90 percent comes directly from the diary and other sources. Passages in italics are direct quotes from Sarah's diary. I hope that young readers will be inspired by Sarah's spirit and buoyant faith, and perhaps examine the diary for themselves one day.

Charles East's support and helpful suggestions have been greatly appreciated. Many thanks go to Father George Kontos of St. James Episcopal Church, and to Mrs. Jo Ann Hackenberg for welcoming us into her beautiful home at Linwood. Thanks also to Brenda Gates for her help and encouragement; and loving gratitude to my husband, Curtis, for his patience. And, finally, special thanks to Stacey, the best research assistant a mom could have.